Plot Twist

A Village Library Mystery, Volume 14

Elizabeth Spann Craig

Published by Elizabeth Spann Craig, 2026.

This is a work of fiction. Similarities to real people, places, or events are entirely coincidental.

PLOT TWIST

First edition. February 17, 2026.

Copyright © 2026 Elizabeth Spann Craig.

ISBN: 978-1955395625

Written by Elizabeth Spann Craig.

In memory of Dan Harris and his 10 years of meticulous beta reading.

Chapter One

The October light coming through my cottage windows had that sort of golden quality that made everything feel like a memory, even when it was happening. I stood at the kitchen counter, watching dust motes drift through the sunbeams, and smiled. In three weeks, I'd marry Grayson Phillips.

Fitz had already claimed the one patch of sunlight not currently blocked by stacked boxes of Grayson's and my combined book collections. Fitz turned twice, kneaded the worn cushion he was lying on, and collapsed with a sigh of satisfaction. The ongoing renovation of my cottage had displaced him from three of his favorite napping spots, but he was adapting. Cats are amazingly resourceful that way.

There was a light tap on my door. I opened it to find Grayson there holding two cups of coffee from Keep Grounded. He handed me my cup, and I took a quick sip. It was exactly the way I wanted it, with perhaps a bit more cream than many people would consider reasonable.

"Good morning," he said, dropping a kiss on my forehead.

"It is," I agreed. And it was. Despite the plastic sheeting dividing the cottage, despite the sawdust that was determined to settle on every surface, despite the unpacked boxes, it was a very good morning. The sunroom was really coming together, as were the other additions. Our book collections would eventually have a proper home. And in a few short weeks, Grayson would be my husband.

The doorbell rang.

"That'll be Vivian," I said, and tried not to let my shoulders tense.

Our wedding planner swept through the door in a cloud of expensive perfume and professional efficiency. Vivian Cross was impeccably dressed, as always in a silk blouse, tailored slacks, and heels that seemed impractical for a visit to what was basically a construction site and probably cost more than my monthly grocery budget. She was already checking her phone as she walked in.

"Darlings!" She air-kissed somewhere in the vicinity of my cheek. "Sorry I'm a few minutes late for our meeting. I was on a call with a vendor in Charlotte." She glanced around the living room, taking in the boxes, the plastic sheeting, and Fitz sprawled in his sunbeam. "Oh my. You're certainly stuck in that transition phase, aren't you?"

"The renovation should be mostly done before the wedding," said Grayson.

"Mostly," Vivian repeated, with a small smile that suggested she'd heard that before and that it had never ended well. She settled herself on the edge of our sofa, perching, as if she might need to make a hasty escape from the chaos. She pulled a thick binder from her oversized bag. "Well. Let's talk about where we are with everything."

Fitz, ever the diplomat, discarded his sunbeam and padded over to investigate our guest. He wound around her ankles once, then looked up fetchingly at her with the expression that usually earned him love from everyone in Whitby.

Vivian drew her feet back. "Oh. No, no." She waved a hand at Fitz as if shooing a fly. "I'm wearing silk. And I'm allergic. Terribly allergic."

She didn't sneeze. Her eyes didn't water. But Fitz got the message. He gave her one long, sad, unblinking look and returned to his sunbeam with his dignity intact. I liked to think I was a good judge of character. But Fitz was better.

I sat across from Vivian with Grayson beside me on the sofa. This was supposed to be a simple check-in and timeline review. Basically, just final confirmations without anything complicated.

Vivian flipped to a tabbed section of her binder. "So. Centerpieces."

"We decided on simple garden arrangements," I said. "Mason jars with wildflowers and greenery. Sarah Chen is handling it." I said this in the tone of someone providing a helpful reminder. But Vivian should certainly know what Sarah was doing.

"Yes, I have that noted. Although I have a florist in Charlotte coming up with another idea for you. It'll just be something to consider. We'll talk about that later. For now, we'll focus on the Mason jars." Vivian pulled out a glossy photograph, sliding across the coffee table toward us. "I wanted to show you an alternative, though. I think it would really elevate the reception. Crystal centerpieces with formal arrangements. Very elegant and sophisticated."

The photograph showed something that looked like it belonged at a black-tie gala, not a backyard wedding in Whitby. Grayson glanced over at me, as if seeing if I wanted to handle it or have him step in.

"That's beautiful," I said carefully. "But it's not really what we're going for."

"I understand. You want 'simple.'" She said the word the way someone might say 'quaint' or 'rustic,' with a particular tone that suggested she was humoring us. "But I've planned dozens of weddings, darling, and I can tell you that brides often regret not going a bit more polished. When I did the Morrison wedding in Charlotte, the bride initially wanted something understated, and I convinced her to trust my vision. The photographs were stunning."

"We really do want simple," Grayson said. His tone was pleasant, but I could hear the firmness underneath. "Garden flowers and mason jars. That's the vision we're looking for."

Vivian's smile didn't waver, but something flickered behind her eyes. "Of course. It's your day." She made a note in her binder. "Though I do hope you'll at least consider the upgraded linens I mentioned last week. The ones you selected are perfectly fine for a backyard gathering, but not for a wedding of this caliber."

"What caliber is that, exactly?" Grayson asked.

I bit back a smile.

Vivian blinked. "Well. You're both professionals. Grayson, you publish and edit the newspaper. Ann, you're a reference librarian. People will be watching and judging you. You want to make the right impression."

"We want to get married in our garden with our friends," I said. "That's the impression we're going for."

Vivian looked back down at her binder. "Of course." She flipped to a new section of the notebook. "Now, about the menu. I spoke with Jasper, and I have some concerns about presentation. The food itself is fine, I suppose. It's very authentic home-style cooking. But I thought perhaps we could discuss some elevated options. A few sophisticated touches would really make a difference."

My head started hurting. "We love Jasper's menu exactly as it is. That's why we hired him."

Vivian looked at me for a long moment. Then she smiled, a professional smile that didn't quite reach her eyes, and closed her binder.

"Very well. I can see you both have a clear vision." The way she said *vision* made it sound like something slightly embarrassing. "We're meeting at Jasper's this afternoon for the final timeline review. I'll see you there?"

"We'll be there," Grayson said.

Vivian gathered her things, her movements brisk and efficient. At the door, she paused and looked back at us. "You know, I only push because I care about giving my clients the best possible day. When you look back at your wedding photos in twenty years, you won't remember wanting 'simple.' You'll only see what you got."

And then she was gone, leaving a faint trace of expensive perfume and the distinct feeling we'd failed some sort of test.

The door clicked shut. Grayson and I looked at each other.

"So, that went well," he said.

I burst out laughing. I couldn't help it. "Crystal centerpieces. She actually brought a picture of crystal centerpieces."

"For a wedding of this caliber," Grayson said, grinning.

"The caliber where we spend three times our budget on things we don't want."

Grayson walked to the kitchen and made a pot of coffee, since we'd finished ours from Keep Grounded. He came back a few minutes later with cups for us both. I accepted mine with a smile. Somehow, Vivian's presence always made me feel like I needed warming up.

"You know," he said, settling beside me on the sofa, "we could still fire her. We're clearly not seeing eye to eye on the vision thing here. The only reason we sprang for a planner was because the minor details were stressing us out. If our *planner* is stressing us out, then we're not accomplishing what we wanted."

I shook my head. "I think it's too late to fire Vivian. She's coordinating four vendors, has deposits in her name, and she's good at logistics. The major issue we have with her is her determination to give us a wedding we're not asking for."

"That's not going to happen," Grayson said. He reached out to squeeze my hand. "We'll make sure we're getting exactly what we want. It's our day, no one else's."

I smiled. He looked quite fierce. I brushed his hair out of his eyes. "You're right. And at least this afternoon should go smoother."

"I can't believe we're meeting her again today."

"At the caterer's venue. But Jasper actually gets what we're looking for, so it should be a straightforward review of what we've already decided."

Fitz, who'd remained magnificently unbothered throughout Vivian's visit, stretched luxuriously in his sunbeam. He had the right idea about how to handle difficult people.

"It's too bad we couldn't meet with Jasper this morning instead," said Grayson. "Then we wouldn't have felt like we were spending the entire day with Vivian."

"I know. But Jasper does some sort of morning walk with hand weights every day. He's apparently very committed to not breaking his streak."

Grayson chuckled. "Right. I keep forgetting the town of Whitby is chockful of characters."

"Covered up with them, yes. Caterers with morning constitutionals," I said with a grin.

"It sounds like a smart way to keep the weight off. After all, he's cooking delicious stuff all the time and presumably has to taste them," said Grayson.

A saw screamed to life somewhere behind the plastic sheeting. Fitz's ears flattened. Then a contractor moved on to what sounded like enthusiastic hammering.

Grayson glanced at his watch. "They're starting pretty early today." He gave me a sympathetic look. "Sorry. I know the construction isn't easy to deal with."

"It's okay. I've gotten very attached to those noise-canceling headphones you bought me. Although I think Fitz could use a pair."

"At least we'll have extra space eventually," said Grayson. "When I talked to one of the guys yesterday, he said they should be wrapping up before the wedding."

"Really?" My tone was more doubtful than hopeful.

"His exact words were 'barring any surprises.' Which, in contractor parlance, I believe means 'probably not.' But we don't have any control over the construction. We can only look forward to the results whenever it's done. We'll have a place to put all our books."

I looked around at the boxes, the plastic sheeting, and the displaced cat now monitoring the construction noise with one suspicious ear. In three weeks, I was marrying a man who brought me coffee fixed exactly right and stood beside me against pushy wedding planners. All the chaos was temporary stuff. The rest of it, the important part, was permanent.

"And Fitz will have his sunroom." I looked over at the cat, who'd closed his eyes against the indignity of sawdust and displacement. "He's been very patient."

Fitz's ear twitched, acknowledging the compliment without opening his eyes.

I frowned. "Uh-oh. I just realized I left my wedding planning notebook at work yesterday."

"Do you need it for the meeting with the caterer?"

I considered this. But nodded. "Unfortunately. We've considered so many different dishes that I'll never be able to make sure we're going with our original plan unless I run by the library and pick up the notebook."

A spate of hammering and drilling made Grayson pause before answering. "Will you be able to get in and get out of there?"

Grayson knew me well, and it was a fair question. The library was both my favorite place and the spot where I had the most challenging time disconnecting from. I was in there so often that my regular patrons would come up for a chat or to ask a question, whether I was working that day or not.

"I think so," I said.

Which was exactly when the construction drove us totally out of the cottage.

Chapter Two

We'd barely made it to the front porch when Zelda Smith, homeowner association president and library volunteer extraordinaire, materialized from the direction of her house. She was moving with the purposeful stride of someone who'd been waiting for exactly this opportunity. Her henna-red hair was particularly vibrant in the morning light, and she had a clipboard tucked under one arm.

"Ann. Grayson." She nodded at each of us in turn. "I was doing my morning walkthrough of the neighborhood."

"Of course you were," I said, keeping my voice pleasant. Zelda's "morning walkthroughs" had a tendency to coincide with any activity she wanted to monitor.

"I couldn't help but notice the crew arrived early today." She pulled out the clipboard, which I now saw contained what appeared to be a detailed log. "They started working at 8:12. That's before the approved construction window of 8:30."

"I'm sorry about that," I said. "I'll mention it to them later today."

"That's very kind of you," said Zelda with a sniff. She looked curiously at the cottage, then affected a nonchalant expression.

"How's the work progressing? Staying within the approved architectural review plans?"

"As far as I know," I said. "Would you like to inspect it?"

Zelda's eyes lit up for a moment before she composed herself. "Well, I wouldn't want to intrude. But since I *am* on the architectural review board, it would be responsible of me to do a periodic check. Just to make sure everything is going according to plan."

"We'd hate for you to be irresponsible," Grayson said. I could hear the smile in his voice, although his expression remained perfectly neutral.

Zelda either missed the gentle teasing or chose to ignore it. "I'll stop by day-after-tomorrow. I have a checkup tomorrow, so it'll have to be the next day. I'll arrive during the approved construction hours." She made another note, then surprised me by tucking her clipboard away and peering at me. "And how are you holding up? You've got a wedding in three weeks, construction chaos, and that wedding planner of yours to deal with."

I blinked. It sounded like genuine concern. And I wasn't entirely sure how she knew about Vivian. "You know our planner?"

"I know she's been coming and going from your cottage at all hours, always looking like she's about to take on the whole town." Zelda sniffed again. "I looked her up online. She used to work the Charlotte circuit. She did big society weddings and that sort of thing."

"That's right."

Zelda said, "Don't let her bulldoze you. She's fully capable of doing that. If you want a simple wedding, you have a simple wedding. It's nobody's day but yours."

It was quite possibly the kindest thing Zelda had ever said to me. "Thanks, Zelda."

"Don't mention it. Literally. I have a crusty reputation to maintain." She turned and headed back down the sidewalk, clipboard tucked firmly under her arm, already scanning the neighboring houses for violations.

Grayson watched her go. "Did Zelda Smith just give you emotional support?"

"I believe she did. The quitting-smoking thing has really mellowed her out."

Grayson said, "Relatively speaking."

"Very relatively speaking."

A few minutes later, I hurried into the library. The familiar smell of old paper and lemon furniture polish settled something in me, even as I scanned the room for Wilson. The coast was clear when I walked in; I didn't see Wilson, my director, or Luna, my friend in the children's section. I ducked behind the reference desk, grabbed my notebook, and then heard a familiar voice and groaned internally. It was Mrs. Sullivan, one of our regular patrons. She was in her seventies, sharp as a tack, and had run the town's most successful real estate office for thirty years. However, she tended to struggle with technology. And technology seemed to be winning the battle.

Mrs. Sullivan strode up to me with the air of someone about to testify before Congress. "Ann, I need your help. The bank is doing it again. They're most annoying."

"You mean the bank's two-factor authentication?"

"If that's what they're calling it now." Mrs. Sullivan set her phone on the desk like evidence in a court case. "I've figured out the issue. The bank sends the code to my phone, but by the time I type it in, it's expired. So clearly, the problem involves my phone receiving the codes too slowly."

"Actually, the codes are ordinarily valid for anywhere from thirty seconds to a minute."

"Precisely! My phone is at least ten seconds behind real time. I've noticed it before. The clock on my microwave is faster. So you and I need to fix my phone." Mrs. Sullivan stared down the offensive device.

I took a steadying breath. "Tell you what. How about if you and I get you into the bank right now?"

Mrs. Sullivan cast a suspicious look at the public computers. "Over there?"

They weren't the most secure devices to do banking on, it was true. "Have you thought about downloading the bank's app?"

She looked at me with great surprise. "No. You mean bank on my phone? Is that a good idea?"

"Usually, it doesn't create too much of a problem. Do you know your login at the bank?"

Amazingly, she did. But then, she'd always had a very sharp mind. She signed in on the site after I downloaded the app, then we waited for the two-factor authentication. It arrived in seconds.

Mrs. Sullivan appeared disgusted by this instead of relieved. "So annoying. The code comes when someone else is waiting for it. It's like it knows it's not me on the other end."

"I know what you mean. It's like taking a car to the garage for a funny noise, then the car behaves perfectly well when the mechanic is listening to it."

But Mrs. Sullivan, eager to get on with her banking business, only murmured a vague reply and wandered off. Crisis solved, I headed again for the door with my notebook. I could hear Wilson speaking with Mona in the background about birdwatching at the Ridgeline Trail near Jasper's farmhouse. Wilson appeared to be talking about warblers passing through and that they needed to be mindful of groundhog holes. He sounded like he was giving a fairly pedantic lecture about groundhog neatness and how they cleaned debris out of their homes. I strode out before I could get noticed and waylaid again.

I spent the rest of the morning the way I always did when I was too restless to sit still; I made myself useful. I ran errands at the drugstore and hardware store. I tried settling into a corner of Keep Grounded with my coffee and Krista Davis's *The Diva Takes the Cake* on my phone. It was a cozy mystery about a wedding that goes terribly wrong. This was perhaps not the wisest choice, given my current circumstances. But Sophie Winson's problems made mine feel much more manageable by comparison. The coffeehouse was entirely too bustling for me to focus. It had to be quieter than at Construction Central, but after twenty minutes I gave up and headed home. My noise-canceling headphones should help with the racket.

But the construction crew was apparently on their lunch break when I got back. I had a blissfully quiet stretch of time to eat a sandwich, answer emails, and snuggle with Fitz, who draped himself across my legs like a warm orange blanket. I very deliberately avoided thinking about crystal centerpieces.

The quiet time did me a world of good, and by the time I met Grayson that afternoon, I was ready to take on the catering.

Jasper's venue was a converted farmhouse on the edge of town, set back from Ridgeline Road down a gravel drive. It had white clapboard, a wraparound porch with rocking chairs, and a faded sign with his name in hand-painted letters. A small parking lot for a nearby trailhead sat right past the property line. I could see a couple of cars there with hikers heading out for the afternoon. It was the trail that Jasper walked early each morning.

Vivian was there early, tapping a high-heeled foot while checking her phone. It was tough to nail the wedding planner's age, but she seemed to be in her late 40s to early 50s. She was slim, carefully maintained, and always impeccably dressed and coiffured.

Grayson pulled up to the farmhouse a second later, giving me a warm smile as he stepped out of the car. Vivian gave a huff of relief that we were there, as if we were quite late instead of ten minutes early. "There you are!" she said. "Let's head inside. We'll want to make absolutely sure Jasper is on-track for the menu we're looking for."

Grayson said in the tone of someone giving a friendly reminder, "Which is simple, Southern cooking."

Vivian acted as if she hadn't heard this. "Jasper said he would come up with a tasting menu."

"We did a tasting menu last time we were here," I said in the tone of someone giving a *not* so friendly reminder.

"Yes, but it doesn't hurt to consider other options," Vivian said brusquely as she pushed open the door to the business.

The kitchen was the heart of the place. It held commercial equipment alongside pieces that looked like they'd been there for generations, like a cast-iron skillet hanging on the wall and a worn wooden cutting board. The whole building smelled of freshly cooked biscuits and slow-cooked barbeque. It was the kind of smell that made you hungry, even if you'd already eaten. I felt a twinge of hunger, even though I'd just had that sandwich. My stomach growled quietly. The farmhouse often hosted events and was well thought-of as a venue. But Grayson and I had planned on having our reception in the backyard of the cottage.

Jasper immediately greeted us. He was a big, laid-back guy sporting a mountain-man beard. Although his size made him look like something of a bruiser, he had a gentleness of manner that totally belied it. "How are y'all doing today?" he asked. His tone indicated he really wanted to know.

"We're fine, fine," said Vivian in the clipped tone of someone who had far more important things to do than chitchat. "What have you got for us today?"

Jasper gave Vivian a thoughtful look, as if trying to figure her out. Her energy level was about twenty times his. He quickly gave up his attempt to figure her out, giving us a wide smile instead. "I've got a detailed menu that I put together from the tasting. I just need for you to give me the serving timeline. Then, at Vivian's request, I've got a few items that could be good alternates, if you feel you'd like to make any changes to what we've set up."

He had the look of someone trying to navigate a particularly dangerous minefield. I felt sorry for him. I wondered how often he found himself caught between Vivian and clients.

Grayson looked at me, as if trying to feel out how I wanted to approach this. I must have looked aggravated, because he stepped right in. "We appreciate the work of coming up with other options, but Ann and I are happy with what we've had planned with you. We'll approve that and go over the timeline."

Vivian broke in. "You might be surprised by some of the elevated options Jasper has. They're a lot more sophisticated than his family recipes, which are charming but perhaps too rustic."

Jasper didn't argue with Vivian, but caught my eye with a knowing look.

I said firmly, "Actually, charmingly rustic is exactly what we're looking for. Besides, it's delicious. This is a backyard wedding with friends." Vivian looked as if she were about to object. I opened my wedding planning notebook to the page where I'd listed our final choices. "Here are our picks for the menu. Now, where's the paperwork? Grayson needs to get back to work, and I have some reading to do on my day off."

Vivian opened her mouth to object before snapping it closed again. Grayson's eyes twinkled as he looked at me.

We approved the serving timeline and the menu and paid another deposit check while we were there.

Vivian was still visibly aggravated and diverted herself by compulsively checking her phone while we took care of our paperwork.

Jasper very kindly packed up the "elevated" samples he'd prepared for us so we could snack on them later. Then we headed for the door. Vivian turned to look over her shoulder at Jasper. "Remember, I'll be back tomorrow morning with a different client for a tasting menu. I'd prefer it if you bring out the elevated menu choices to present to them. I think they're the sort who'd want them." With that, she flounced out the door.

Before Grayson and I left, Jasper said, "Hey, since y'all like my cooking so much, you should stop by tomorrow morning around eight-thirty, after I'm back from my walk. You might want to try my grandma's biscuits when they're fresh out of the oven. They're best eaten warm with honey butter or apple butter."

I was about to turn down the opportunity because I knew I was working the next morning. But I stopped myself. Why not? The process of planning the wedding hadn't been as fun as I'd hoped for, and these little pockets of pleasure should be something I sought out. "Actually, that would be amazing. I'll be here." I turned to Grayson. "What's your schedule like tomorrow?"

He gave a regretful shake of his head. "I've got an interview I'm doing first thing. I'm sorry I'll be missing out. Those biscuits sound awesome."

We walked outside, where Vivian gave us a quick wave and then hopped in her large SUV and sped off. Grayson grinned at me. "We're not the sort who'd want elevated choices."

"I always did wonder what was wrong with us," I said with a grin. "I'm glad Vivian helped me figure it out." I opened my car door, leaning on it. "Where are you off to now? Back to the office?"

Grayson was the editor of the Whitby newspaper, a job that had some flexibility, but also consumed large amounts of his time. He pulled a face. "Sadly, I have a meeting with an advertiser."

"That doesn't exactly sound under your remit as editor."

Grayson nodded. "Yeah, our marketing guy has been out a lot lately and we want to get this advertiser locked down. I offered to go in his place." He reached out, giving me a warm hug. "I'll check in with you later today."

The next morning, dressed with a sense of purpose, determined to enjoy some good Southern biscuits before heading into the library. Fitz watched me curiously as I headed for the door. I tickled him under his fuzzy chin. "I'll be back to get you before I drive to the library. But I've got something to do first."

Fitz looked solemnly at me, as if he understood every word. Then he curled up again and faded back to sleep as I headed out the door.

It was a clear, chilly morning with a few fluffy clouds making swift progress across the blue sky. I turned onto Ridgeline Road, already anticipating the warm kitchen at the farmhouse. The trailhead parking lot was empty, which surprised me a little. Usually, it was a popular spot for hikers, even on a cool, breezy morning.

I did see a car in Jasper's parking lot, though, and winced, recognizing Vivian's vehicle. I remembered she was supposed to be meeting another client for a tasting. It might be a short and sweet biscuit treat for me then, unless Vivian was completely focused on her other client and not on taking another opportuni-ty to convince me to upgrade my catering.

I heard someone whistling an old tune that sounded like it might be an off-pitch version of "Old Susanna" and saw Jasper walking briskly down the Ridgeline trail, gripping hand weights. He grinned apologetically at me. "Sorry, have you been waiting long? I took a quick walk while the biscuits were baking. They should be ready to pull out of the oven now."

He frowned when he saw Vivian's empty SUV. "Looks like she must have walked inside to wait." He sighed. "I think of my-self as a pretty patient person, but she really tests that some-times. And she's always complaining that I'm late, but I'm not. She's simply here twenty minutes early all the time. She knows my schedule."

I gave Jasper a sympathetic look. "She's not the easiest per-son to deal with."

"Nope," he said cheerfully. "But she does seem good at her job. She's organized, anyway. Come on in and have a biscuit, and we'll brave Vivian together."

But when we walked inside, there was no need to brave Vi-vian after all. She was lying face-down on the floor, with a heavy catering tray next to her.

Chapter Three

Jasper ran up to check for a pulse while I called 911, requesting an ambulance and police. Jasper turned to look at me, shaking his head. "She's gone." His gaze rested on the tray next to her and closed his eyes briefly.

"We should step out," I said. "This is a crime scene."

We walked outside, Jasper turning to look back at Vivian before we left the farmhouse. "I can't believe it," he said as he followed me out to the parking lot.

"The police are on their way." I paused. "You didn't see Vivian before you set out for your walk?"

"No. No, I didn't." Jasper ran a hand through his hair. "I got to the farmhouse early, started the biscuits in the oven, then I grabbed my hand weights and headed to the trail. I don't even know what she was doing here."

"Yesterday, she reminded you about a client tasting."

Jasper said, "Sure, but that should have been later. Vivian knows I'm baking early."

"Wasn't she always early, though?"

Jasper gave a shaky laugh. "Well, that's true. She always showed up way before she was supposed to. It was annoying, frankly. I mean, you don't want people to be late, but you don't want people to be *that* early. It messes you up either way." He shook his head. "Why is she dead? And why is she dead in my business?"

The police and ambulance were pulling in right as he was finishing his sentence. Burton, our police chief and a friend of mine, hopped out, looking grim. A few minutes later, an officer strung up crime scene tape, and Burton walked over to join us. "What happened?" he asked.

Jasper took a deep breath. "I'm not sure. I arrived over here around 6:30 and got organized for the day, checked my calendar, and stuff like that. Then I whipped up some biscuits, which I put into the oven." His eyes opened wide. "I totally forgot to take them out of the oven just now."

Burton called to one of the uniformed police to do so. The man hurried off. "Okay," said Burton. "So you made the biscuits. Then Vivian showed up."

Jasper shook his head. "I never saw Vivian this morning. She must have arrived when I was out taking my walk on the Ridge-line Trail."

Burton frowned. "So you left food in the oven."

"Briefly. I always have a morning walk after I get here. I need the exercise, and it sort of resets me, too."

"Do you have any idea why Vivian was here this morning?" asked Burton.

"Well, we were supposed to have a tasting for one of her clients, but that was a little later. Vivian always showed up early, though. I guess she'd come out especially early this morning."

Burton said, "Did anyone else see you this morning? Anyone who can verify you were on your walk?"

"No. I was by myself. Just out on the trail with my weights."

"No one can verify exactly when you left the building or returned," said Burton.

Jasper turned eagerly to me. "Ann and I walked into the farmhouse together. She knows when I came back. She called you as soon as we found Vivian."

"Right. But you could have come back from your walk earlier then waited for Ann to 'witness' you returning."

Jasper turned pale.

Burton said, "Tell me a little about Vivian. What was she like?"

Jasper took another deep breath. His voice was shaky now. "She was pretty difficult to deal with. But very professional. Vivian knew exactly what she wanted, and she was clear about a vendor's responsibility for providing it."

Burton said, "How did the vendors view her?"

"She wasn't anybody's favorite. She could be very demanding. Vivian's standards were very high." Jasper paused. "She could be pushy with her clients, too. It wasn't only her vendors. She wanted everybody to choose the best. Sometimes Vivian had a different vision for weddings than her clients did."

Burton looked thoughtful at this. "Can you think of anyone specifically?"

"Not really. It was everyone." Jasper turned to look at me. "Ann probably feels the same way. Vivian was always pushing for the perfect, expensive, big-budget wedding."

Burton turned to look at me. I nodded. "He's right. She was pushy with Grayson and me, too."

"But she didn't deserve this," said Jasper. "No one deserves this."

Burton said, "Can you think of anyone who's had an especially rough time with Vivian lately? Anyone in particular?"

Jasper considered his, running a hand through his hair again. "Look, I'm not trying to make anyone a suspect, here. This is a small town. I'm trying to run a business that depends a lot on everyone around me. The vendors work almost like a team, even though we represent different areas."

"I understand that," said Burton. "But if you have anything useful in helping us track down who did this to Vivian, you need to share it."

Jasper hesitated. "Sarah Chen. She's the florist here. She's had a rough time with Vivian lately. I mean, we all *usually* have a tough time with her, but Vivian has especially been on her case."

"What kind of trouble are we talking about with Sarah Chen?" asked Burton.

"I only know what Sarah told me. We were having a gripe-fest about Vivian on the phone recently. She told me she lost two clients because Vivian called Sarah's floral designs 'provincial' right in front of the brides. It happened twice in a month. Sarah said she couldn't afford to keep losing clients because of Vivian." Jasper looked guilty. "Look, that's not enough to *murder* somebody. It was just Sarah letting off steam."

"And you were letting off steam, too," added Burton.

"Sure I was. Vivian was annoying. But there's a difference between being aggravated with someone and wanting to kill them."

Burton asked, "Did you witness any direct confrontation between Sarah and Vivian? Or only the phone call?"

Jasper hesitated. "No, I didn't see any kind of confrontation. But I know Vivian had a really awful effect on Sarah. One day last month, Sarah was here at the farmhouse, and Vivian walked in. Sarah froze up, and her face went totally white."

Burton nodded and made a couple of notes in a small notebook. "Okay. Look, I know this is inconvenient, but I'm going to need you to stay away from the farmhouse for today and probably tomorrow, too. We're going to need to process the scene and get forensics here and the state police, too. Just head back home, run errands, whatever you need to do. But stay available by phone in case I have more questions."

Burton turned to me. "I'll be in touch." He paused. "And I'm sorry about your wedding. I hope you can figure something out."

"Thanks, Burton."

As Burton headed toward the farmhouse, Jasper and I walked toward the gravel parking lot and our cars.

Jasper looked at me with concern. "Are you holding up okay? That was a tough thing for us to walk into."

"I'm still processing it. How about you?"

Jasper nodded. "Yeah. That was the last thing I expected when I was heading in to get biscuits out." He leaned against his truck. "I guess I'm taking a day or two off."

"Is that going to put you behind?"

"It will, but it can't be helped," said Jasper. "At least I don't have any big events for a few days." He frowned. "It's probably going to impact you a lot more."

"Maybe, but I feel bad even thinking about the wedding when Vivian's dead." It was hard to believe Vivian was gone. She was such a big personality.

Jasper said, "Your wedding is in, what, a few weeks?"

"That's right."

Jasper said, "It's enough time to sort out backup plans. But I'm sorry." He shook his head. "You know, if I'd been here at the farmhouse instead of out walking, maybe there's something I could have done."

"Or maybe you'd be dead too, Jasper. You can't think about what-ifs."

"You're right," said Jasper. He looked at his watch. "It's still the start of the day. It feels like it should be suppertime or something. Ann, let me know if you need anything. And tell Grayson I said hey."

Jasper headed off, and I climbed into my car. It was an overcast day, which matched my mood. I wondered if Grayson was in the middle of something important at work. He'd had a lot of staff issues at the newspaper and always seemed to be filling in. But then, he told me to call him whenever, that he'd call me back if he was stuck. So I took him at his word. I sat in my car so I wouldn't have to drive and chat while I was already so distracted.

"Hey Ann," he said warmly. "I was just thinking about you."

"I was thinking about you, too."

There must have been something odd about my voice because Grayson immediately said, "Is everything okay?"

"Unfortunately, no. Vivian is dead."

"Vivian our wedding planner?" Grayson's voice had rapidly changed into something serious and focused.

"Yes. I was meeting up with Jasper for biscuits at the farmhouse, and we walked in to find her dead on the floor. She was murdered, Grayson. There was a serving tray on the floor next to her."

Grayson asked, "Where are you now? Do you need me to come get you?"

"No, I'm okay. I was kind of shaken up at first, though. I'm sitting in the parking lot at Jasper's right now, but I'm going to drive home after I finish talking with you."

"I can come and meet you," said Grayson quickly.

"You've been slammed at work. There's no need. Although, from a completely different angle, you're probably going to want to write this story up."

Grayson said, "Right. I'll get in touch with Burton. Actually, I'll probably change some of my plans around today and get over to the farmhouse." He paused. "I'm sorry about Vivian. I know she was difficult, but she didn't deserve this."

"No, she didn't."

"Remind me what your day looks like," Grayson said. "You're working this afternoon, right? Was there anything else you had scheduled, or can you take a break?"

"I'm at the library this afternoon. I was originally supposed to have an appointment with Vivian at Sarah Chen's later this morning." I remembered what Jasper had said about Vivian's interactions with the florist and about Sarah's resulting lost income. I'd informally contacted Sarah about doing our flowers at the wedding before we'd hired Vivian as a planner. Then Vivian had taken it upon herself to make arrangements with a florist in Charlotte to 'elevate' the event. I wasn't sure whether Vivian had canceled this appointment with Sarah or not.

"Oh, right, Sarah." Grayson was quiet for a moment. "Let's make sure she's still on track for doing our flowers. We wanted everything low-key and definitely don't need somebody from Charlotte doing the arrangements."

"You're right. I'll give her a call. I guess I shouldn't tell her what happened to Vivian because Burton might want to tell her in person and gauge her reaction."

Grayson's voice was curious now. "Really? Why, is she a suspect?"

"It sounds like Burton will want to talk to her, given what Jasper told me. She and Vivian have had some run-ins lately. Anyway, I'll be careful with what I say."

"Got it. I'll wrap up here as early as I can this afternoon. Do you want to have supper at your place tonight? I'll bring the food."

"That would be amazing, thanks," I said.

"Ann? I love you."

"I love you, too." I hung up and took a breath. I felt marginally more human. I was about to look up the florist's number just to make sure she was still on for our wedding. But then I decided I'd go over in person. Maybe I could find out more about Sarah Chen's issues with Vivian. Or, at the very least, get more of a handle on what had made my wedding planner tick.

But first, I wanted to go home and completely reset. Maybe cuddle with Fitz a little. I crossed my fingers that the construction work wouldn't be too over-the-top, although I'd definitely gotten used to the noise-canceling headphones.

But when I walked inside the cottage, I was delighted to find the guys leaving my house in order to pick up something they needed from a warehouse. Perfect timing. Fitz, who seemed to like the contractors individually, but not collectively, looked relieved. I made myself a cup of chai tea, wrapping my hands around the warm mug, and settled with Fitz on the sofa for a while. The spices helped. So did the quiet and Fitz's purring.

It was late-morning when the construction started up again. I took that as my sign it was time to move along. I hopped into the car and set off for the flower shop.

Chapter Four

Sarah Chen's place was a small storefront downtown. The door chimed as I pushed it open, and the cool, damp air hit me immediately. It was that florist shop atmosphere of refrigerated cases and fresh-cut stems. I smelled roses over greenery, with something a little sharper underneath. Eucalyptus, maybe.

Sarah was at the worktable at the back, talking on the phone, which was tucked between her shoulder and ear. She was busily stripping leaves from a pile of stems. "No, the blush, not the coral. There's a big difference. I'll have them ready by four." She hung up, looking over at me. "Hey, Ann. Give me one second."

She finished the stem she was working on and wiped her hands on her apron. The shop was cluttered in the way of someone doing everything herself. There were buckets of flowers everywhere, spools of ribbon, and a stack of invoices that were held down by a rock that might have been decorative or might have simply been a rock.

"Sorry about that," she said, from behind a table. "The mother of the bride keeps changing her mind about the boutonnieres." She smiled at me. "How's it going?" Sarah was in her early thirties with a quiet prettiness. Her dark hair was pulled back into a ponytail, with a few strands escaping.

I said, "Hey there. I wanted to make sure we were still on for flowers for Grayson's and my wedding."

"That would be amazing. I wasn't sure where we stood. Vivian canceled our appointment. She told me you might be considering a different approach a florist in Charlotte was working on."

"That doesn't totally surprise me. But Grayson and I would love for you to go with the small arrangements in the Mason jars that we discussed earlier."

"Great. I was looking forward to doing it. Simple flowers can really make a wedding beautiful." Then Sarah's face shifted to an expression I couldn't quite read. "Listen, I heard what happened with Vivian. It's shocking. I'm so sorry—I know she was your wedding planner."

This seemed fast, even for Whitby. "How did you hear the news?"

"Another vendor stopped by Jasper's place and saw all the police cars. He asked one of the officers what was going on," said Sarah.

I hoped word wouldn't get out before Vivian's family was notified. I knew she had an ex-husband who lived in Whitby. "I see," I said. I paused. "Vivian could be tricky to work with. I wanted to make sure you understood that Vivian's plan to schedule flowers with a florist in Charlotte was her idea, not mine."

Sarah's face flushed. "It sounds like Vivian. I'm sorry you had a tough time with her. You're not the only one of Vivian's clients who did. I couldn't stand her. I really couldn't stand her. I hate to admit it, but it's the truth." She gave a short laugh. "I even had a public argument with her a couple of weeks ago, at the farmer's market, of all places."

"What was that about?"

Sarah said, "Vivian called my work 'amateur hour.' She said I was costing her clients because I made her events look 'provincial.'"

I shook my head. "That's not true. You do a great job with everything you take on."

Sarah took a steadying breath. "Sorry. I shouldn't have said anything, especially considering what just happened to Vivian. But it's been really hard to shake off what she said."

She gestured to a small framed photograph on the wall near the register. It showed an older woman standing in a garden, surrounded by flowers. "My mom taught me everything she knew about flowers before she passed. And her mom had taught her. I used to sit on my grandmother's porch in the summers and help her make arrangements for the church." Sarah's voice softened. "So that's three generations of women that understood flowers don't have to be expensive to be beautiful. Then Vivian dismissed all that in one word. Provincial."

"That was completely unfair of her."

Sarah shrugged, but I could see the hurt underneath. "I know I don't have formal training like those city florists. I don't have a design degree or a Manhattan apprenticeship. But I grew up in my mom's garden. I know how flowers blend together and how colors work with each other. Surely that's got to count for something." She paused. "I don't know. Maybe 'wildflower charm' isn't really professional enough. I thought natural beauty meant something."

"Of course it does. Did Vivian cost you a lot of work?"

Sarah said, "At least two weddings that I know of. And she almost cost me yours."

I shook my head. "Grayson and I were never going to go along with her plan for the Charlotte florist. But I know any lost weddings must hurt."

"They hurt a lot. It's an enormous loss of revenue for a shop my size." Sarah smiled at me. "Your wedding was going to be a great way to prove that Vivian's way wasn't the only way. You and Grayson wanted simple and natural. You trusted my vision. Now, of course, Vivian's gone and there's nothing I need to prove to her or to anyone." She must have realized how it sounded because she said, "I never wanted anything to happen to Vivian, though. She was just an annoying business associate."

She frowned. "Did you hear anything about what happened to Vivian? Was she in some kind of car accident at Jasper's place?"

I hesitated. But if the information wasn't out yet, it soon would be. "The police seem to be treating it like a suspicious death." As you do when someone has blunt force trauma from a heavy catering tray. I carefully left out the fact that I was there.

Sarah drew in a sharp breath. "Oh no. She was murdered?"

"That's something the police are looking into, I think."

She closed her eyes briefly. She seemed to realize, a beat too late, how her earlier venting might sound. The flush crept back up her neck. "Then they're sure to come talk to me. It's no secret that Vivian and I weren't exactly friends." When she opened her eyes again, there was anxiety there. "Look, I didn't like Vivian, but you know I'd never do anything to hurt her. I wasn't even in town earlier today. I made an early drive to the flower market in Ashville."

"You'll be able to tell the police that, then."

But Sarah frowned. "Well, I was by myself. It's an hour drive each way, and I left before dawn. I paid cash, like I always do, since the wholesale guys give a better deal that way. It doesn't sound like much of an alibi." She picked up a rose stem, then set it down again. "The guy I paid for the flowers barely looked at me because he was on his phone the whole time. Ugh. What am I supposed to do now?"

"Just give Burton a call and get ahead of it. He's always really fair."

Sarah nodded. "Yeah, being proactive sounds like a good idea. And I wasn't the only one who had a tough time with Vivian. It's not like she didn't get on anyone else's bad side. Her ex-husband, for example."

"That's right. I remember Vivian was divorced."

Sarah said with relief, "Exactly. And spouses are always the main suspects, aren't they? Not that they were still married. But an ex has to come pretty close."

"Was there anyone else Vivian had a tough time with lately? That you know of?"

Sarah was quiet for a moment, thinking. "There's Patricia Holbrook."

That was a name I was familiar with from the library since Patricia attended one of our book clubs there. As well, she was another wedding planner. Grayson and I had briefly considered using Patricia until Vivian sold us on her planning services. "Vivian had run-ins with the other wedding planner?"

"That's what Patricia has told me. And I know Vivian had plenty of clients who weren't happy with their weddings, too. So there should be plenty of other suspects." Sarah sounded relieved at the prospect.

I looked at my watch. "I'd better go. I've got work starting soon, and I should grab a bite of lunch first."

"Thanks for coming by, Ann. And for putting your trust in me and my arrangements."

The construction crew was in full force when I got back home for lunch. I ended up taking a sandwich outside with me, enjoying the fall sunshine, despite a brisk breeze that scattered leaves in all directions. The bread was good, the ham was salty, and for ten minutes, nothing was wrong. Then I changed for work, collected Fitz, and headed for the library. It always felt good to be there. After all, the library was my happy place with its tall windows, that particular creak of the old wooden floors, and the hushed conversations. I could use that right about now.

When I walked into the library with the cat carrier, no fewer than ten toddlers came galloping up to see Fitz. I managed to have them all sit in a circle, a feat in itself, before letting him out of the crate. Fortunately, Fitz is the most laid-back cat that ever was, as evidenced by the way he sat in the middle of the circle and allowed toddlers to pet him in turn ("gently! Gently!" I kept saying.)

Their mothers came to collect them all a few moments later, and Fitz trotted off to a sunbeam in the periodicals, where he flopped onto his side and began grooming one paw with great concentration. He might have gone to that area to check on Linus, one of his favorite patrons, as well as mine.

Luna gave me a frazzled look when I joined her in the children's section. "Clearly, I just gave a toddler storytime. Was Fitz traumatized?"

"As if! You know how he is. He loved every minute of the attention. Although I think he's gone looking for Linus and a sunbeam now. Or possibly Linus *in* a sunbeam."

"Good," said Luna. She was re-shelving picture books with slightly manic energy.

"I think there's glitter in your hair. Is that on purpose?" It was a fair question. Luna was fond of doing interesting things to her hair, although it usually was limited to dyeing it various hues. I didn't mention the fact that she appeared to have a hand-puppet dragon on one arm.

"Glitter? Absolutely not. We had a craft that went horribly wrong after storytime. I'm not sure what I was thinking. Toddlers and glitter? I must have been out of my mind." She frowned at the shelf in front of her. "Do you know how many copies of *The Very Hungry Caterpillar* we own? Because I found three under the beanbag chairs. And someone seems to have taken a bite out of this one."

I grinned at her. "No idea. Sounds like a rough hour."

"We had six more toddlers than expected. Six! And someone's well-meaning grandmother brought a bag of rhythm instruments to share. Shakers, triangles, and cowbells. *Cowbells,* Ann." Luna looked down and finally noticed the dragon puppet on her arm. She wrestled it off. "I tried to re-establish some semblance of order for an hour."

The idea of Luna having anything to do with a semblance of order made me grin again.

"And Wilson kept walking by and sighing. Like it was my fault that someone brought noisemakers to a toddler storytime." She made a face. "I hope your morning has been better." She stopped short, suddenly studying my features and frowning. "Actually, I don't think it has been, has it?" she asked slowly. "Spill it. What's happened? It's nothing to do with Grayson, is it?"

"No, nothing with Grayson."

Luna nodded. "I figured. Grayson is always the perfect gentleman. Is it your heinous wedding planner? She hasn't completely tried to hijack your wedding, has she? The last I heard, she had her manicured clutches in your flower arrangements."

I gave Luna a quick rundown of my day so far. She completely stopped re-shelving picture books and gaped at me in astonishment. She said in a loud whisper, "Vivian was murdered?"

"That's right."

Luna gave a low whistle. "Wow. From what you told me, she might have had plenty of people upset with her in town, from a business standpoint alone."

"Yeah. And I understand her personal life was also sort of knotty."

Luna said, "So there are plenty of suspects. Wow. And I thought *I* had a rough morning." She frowned. "But seriously, Ann, what are you going to do? You're into the final stretch before the wedding. And now you don't have a planner."

"Oh, I think Grayson and I can muddle through. Maybe we should have planned it ourselves all along. It seemed like it would be easier on both of us to get a planner, since we're both working."

Luna's eyes grew wide. "Hey, I could help you with planning! I'd love to tackle a fun event like a wedding. And Mom and Wilson aren't letting me get involved with their own wedding planning."

My mind immediately went to the disastrous toddler story-time, a middle school program that devolved into a food fight under Luna's supervision, and other events Luna had planned. "It's okay, really. At this point, most of the planning is done and we're down to execution. But thanks."

Luna was opening her mouth, possibly to debate me on this point, when a young mom juggling two small children walked up to ask her to log her into one of the kid computers. I took the opportunity to head over to the reference desk. Maybe Luna wouldn't remember to follow-up with me later on wedding planning.

Chapter Five

I'd only just gotten started with working on a grant applica-tion for library programming funds when I heard someone give a small cough in front of me. I looked up to see Mrs. Sullivan, she of the two-factor issues. She marched up to the desk where I was stationed, carrying her tablet like a weapon. She had the air of someone about to file a formal complaint.

"Ann, I need your help with this two-factor nonsense. My bank is about to lock me out yet again."

This was sounding like a repeat of our last interaction. "Are you using the bank app we downloaded?" I was careful to say 'we,' not 'I,' but it might as well have been the 'royal we' because Mrs. Sullivan had decidedly not helped with the download. In fact, I'd rather gotten the impression that she opposed it.

She frowned. "Oh, that's right. The app. I don't think that's going to help with the two-factor, though."

"No, it's more of a user experience thing."

Mrs. Sullivan made a scoffing sound at this.

"Let's try again. Did you get a code on your phone the last time?" I asked.

"Yes, and I typed it in correctly. The problem isn't on *my* end. I ran a real estate office for thirty years. I can certainly handle a six-digit number. But it said the code was expired when I put it in. Ridiculous. The bank insists on sending me defective codes."

I said, "Did you type in the code before a minute was up? You have to type them in quickly."

"Yes, yes, I remember what you told me last time. I was well within the window. The problem is clearly on the bank's end." She scowled. "And who decided thirty seconds was sufficient time? I'd like to speak to them."

"I don't think we can contact the people who invented two-factor authentication."

Mrs. Sullivan sniffed. "Then they should have consulted someone with practical experience before implementing such a silly system."

It sounded like Mrs. Sullivan had one more try before getting locked out. I had no idea if why she had so much banking business, but the next try was going to be important. To Mrs. Sullivan, at least. "Let's try it again, this time with the app. We'll get a new code, copy-paste it or type it in quickly, then see what happens."

Naturally, it all went according to plan. Mrs. Sullivan was satisfied, although not convinced the issue was solved. "It worked this time. However, I certainly don't trust it. I'll be back when it locks me out again."

"I'll be here. And good luck with it."

I had a stretch of quiet after that, which enabled me to finish the grant work, tackle some work on a genealogy project a patron had asked me to help with, and work on the library newsletter, which was sprinkled liberally with photos of Fitz, looking fetching as always.

Feeling like I needed to stretch after all the desk work, I stood and walked over to Linus, who was sitting in his usual spot in the periodicals section, peering at the *New York Times*. He put the paper down when he saw me coming.

"How's everything going today?" I asked him.

Linus gave me a wry look in return. "I'm a little sleepy for some reason, so I'm trying to stay awake. I might need to go home for caffeine before trying again with my reading."

"Didn't sleep well last night?"

Linus said, "Not as well as I should have. Ivy has a new habit, and I'm not entirely sure how I feel about it."

Ivy was Linus's rescue dog. She'd been a stray who'd one day shown up at the library, looking confused, hungry, and in need of help. Linus and she had fallen in love with each other. Now Ivy was woven into Linus's daily routine. "What's she doing?"

Linus rubbed his eyes. "She's wanting to sleep in the bed with me. Before, I'd always shut the bedroom door when I turned in. But she's started whining at the door if it's closed. I opened it last night, and she ran in, pleased as punch."

"Did she jump on the bed right away?"

Linus said, "No, she was very polite about it all. You know what a sweetheart she is. She lay down in a corner of the room, very quietly. As if she just wanted to share the space with me and nothing more. I fell asleep, but woke up when she started dreaming."

I grinned. "Was Ivy chasing rabbits in her sleep?"

"Apparently. I suspect the rabbits lost the battle. Anyway, I eventually managed to fall back asleep. But when I woke up again, Ivy was sprawled across the bed on her back, snoring." Linus looked as if he weren't entirely sure what he thought about this turn of events.

"Maybe you could get her a comfy dog bed for the corner of the room?" I suggested. "That might keep her from getting on the bed with you."

Linus smiled at me. "Thank you, Ann. I'll try that." He hid a yawn behind his hand. "She was so happy that I hated kicking her off the bed. But she's something of a bed-hog. I found myself curled up in a tiny ball on the edge of the mattress."

"Well, give the dog bed a go and see what happens." I paused. "Of course, I'm not exactly one to talk. Fitz is usually either curled against my side or on my legs when I sleep."

"He's a bit smaller than Ivy, though."

I nodded. "True."

Linus yawned again, then quickly apologized. "So sorry. I think I will go home to get coffee and lunch. I'll have to be a lot sharper than this if I'm going to play chess this afternoon."

"Oh, is your friend coming by the library to play with you? What's his name again?"

Linus said, "Harold. Yes, we're on for three-thirty. But he's quite sharp and I'll need to make sure I'm not falling asleep over the chess pieces." He carefully stood up, stretching slightly as if he'd gotten stiff. "I'll see you later, Ann."

It was hours later when I finished helping a patron and spotted Linus sitting at a round table with his chessboard and looking lost. I glanced at my watch and saw it was nearly four o'clock. I walked over.

"Harold hasn't shown?"

Linus shook his head. "It's rather odd. Harold is always so prompt."

"Have you tried calling him?"

Linus said, "I texted. I didn't want to interrupt him if he was in the middle of something." He frowned. "I do hope he's all right."

"I'm sure he's probably fine. Maybe he got caught up with something and lost track of the time. It can happen to anyone." I hesitated. From what I'd seen, Harold was an elderly man. I wondered if I should ask Burton to do a wellness check. "Should we check in on Harold?"

Linus looked conflicted. Just then, his phone buzzed, and he lit up. "This is probably Harold, now. He might have been as sleepy as I am. This is what retirement is like sometimes. Stumbling from one nap to another." He pulled out his phone and read the text. "Oh. This is from his daughter, responding to my text. They're at the hospital. Harold fell." His face creased with worry.

"I'm sorry to hear that. But I'm sure he's in good hands."

Linus nodded. "It's worrying, though, falls. I try to keep my phone on me in case anything happens."

I said carefully, not wanting to step out of line, "There are always those medic alert devices, in case your phone is too cumbersome. They have the kind that's on a watch band and one on a lanyard."

"True," said Linus with a sigh. "I'm afraid one of those might be the next step." Now he looked thoroughly unhappy. I'd have sat down to play chess with him, but the library was buzzing with activity, as it usually did after school let out.

Thinking about school gave me a quick idea. "Have you tried playing chess with Timothy? Or Owen?" Timothy was a high school student who was heavily involved with the library, and Owen was a younger boy who also spent a good deal of time here.

A flicker of interest passed across Linus's features. "I haven't. But the kids all have video games and whatnot. I didn't think they'd be interested in something like chess."

"You should let them give it a go. There are lots of young people who love chess. Maybe they already know how to play. If not, I bet they'd be quick to pick it up."

Linus hesitated, looking a little shy.

"Actually, I saw both of them over in the computer section a few minutes ago. How about if I see if they're busy right now? I needed to ask Timothy about our next tech day at the library, anyway."

Linus considered this. "If it's not too much trouble, Ann. Yes, that would be great."

It turned out Timothy and Owen weren't busy and were interested in the game.

Timothy said, "My dad tried to teach me a long time ago, but I didn't catch on. Anyway, he wasn't the most patient guy out there."

I knew Timothy's parents were now divorced. Owen said he didn't know how to play at all. So both kids were happy to join up with Linus and the chessboard. Whenever I glanced over from the reference desk that afternoon, they all looked happily absorbed in the game.

I closed up the library that night and then headed back home with Fitz in tow. The cottage was quiet with the construction crew long gone. I'd changed into a soft top and pants when Grayson, as promised, showed up minutes later with takeout from Quittin' Time for both of us. The smell of warm food filled the kitchen as he gave me a tight hug in greeting.

"I wasn't sure what you wanted, so I ordered burgers and fries for both of us. I hope that's okay," said Grayson.

"Perfect," I said. "I could use some protein. I feel like I'm dragging, and it's definitely not time to turn in yet."

"Considering the morning you had, you have every reason to be dragging."

We dug into the food, which was as reliably comforting as meals usually were from Quittin' Time.

"Were you able to find out anything from Burton?" I asked.

"He confirmed it was blunt force trauma with the tray as the weapon. But he's asking us not to release that information, only to say the police are investigating the death as suspicious." Grayson gave me a regretful look. "Hey, I'm sorry I wasn't with you this morning. It must have been awful finding Vivian."

"It's okay; I was with Jasper. Of course, it was really shocking. You and I just saw Vivian yesterday."

Grayson nodded. "Yeah. It's hard to imagine she's gone. Vivian was something of a force of nature."

"Exactly. It looked to me like she'd been struck from behind with the tray. She was lying on her front. I'm guessing she never saw her attacker." I was quiet for a few moments. "It makes me feel a little better, in some ways. At least she wasn't scared at the end. But it's tough to believe someone hated her enough to strike her down like that."

"I know," said Grayson. "What did Jasper say? After you both found Vivian?"

"Burton was really pressing him for where he'd been this morning. I guess he was trying to understand the exact timing of Vivian's death."

Grayson said, "What did Jasper tell him? Had he even gone into the farmhouse prior to the two of you finding Vivian?"

"Yes, he'd been there early to put the biscuits in the oven. Then he told Burton he'd set off on his walk. He'd joined up with me when he came off the trail, with weights in his hands."

"Okay," said Grayson. "So he was gone when Vivian was murdered."

"Burton was pushing him on that point. Of course, I guess Jasper could have murdered Vivian, stepped out, then waited for me to arrive before walking up with me to the farmhouse. It's not as if anyone was walking with him on the trail. He doesn't have a really solid alibi."

"I see," said Grayson.

"Jasper did mention that Vivian and Sarah Chen had words lately. Well, it was more Vivian having issues with Sarah than the other way around. But I think we'll find the same for anyone who worked with Vivian. It sounds like she was always prickly."

"And a major perfectionist," said Grayson. "I'm sure her customers probably appreciated that to some degree."

"It's nice to know someone has the planning under control, especially when weddings have so many moving parts. But Vivian also created a lot of unnecessary conflict and drama. And she tended to belittle businesses that didn't match her standards."

"We saw that in action a few times," Grayson said wryly. "So how did your visit with Sarah go?"

"She was excited to be back on board for doing our flowers. And she admitted she'd had a lot of problems with Vivian. Apparently, she'd called Sarah's arrangements 'provincial.'"

"Sounds like Vivian," said Grayson, shaking his head. He paused. "Now, a slight change of subject. We just lost our wedding planner."

"Right." I was quiet for a moment. "Honestly, after all we went through with Vivian, I'd rather finish up the wedding planning ourselves. The whole idea behind using a planner was to make the process less stressful. But we didn't really accomplish that with Vivian."

"Definitely not. She was so combative with all the vendors. Plus, she wanted everything her way. Vivian didn't do a great job listening to us."

I nodded. "Exactly. And, at this point, nearly everything is in place. We have the caterer planned, the flowers planned, and the venue is at the cottage. Is it okay with you if we handle the rest of it?"

"Absolutely." He gave me a serious look. "But, if it gets too much, we have options. We can simplify the wedding even more. We can postpone it, if we need to. Or we can even elope."

I gave him a rueful smile. "There's something about eloping that sounds especially appealing right now, I'll admit. And simplification. But I'm definitely not postponing it. I've waited long enough to marry you."

He smiled back at me. "Okay. We'll handle it together."

Chapter Six

The next morning, I blissfully slept in. Fitz was curled up beside me in a ball. He gave me a sleepy look and stretched languorously with a huge yawn that made me laugh. I rubbed his soft fur back down from where it was standing on end. "Good morning. We're sleepy heads today."

Fitz gave me a satisfied feline smile, as if that had been all his idea.

"I wonder why there isn't any construction noise," I said.

Fitz looked as if he didn't care to find out. He was simply enjoying the lack of racket.

I pulled out my phone and checked my email. Sure enough, there was a message from our contractor that the crew had finished with the framing on the sunroom addition and passed the structural inspection. Now I was smiling. The noisiest part of the work was behind us. There would still be drywall, electrical, and finishing to do, but it wouldn't involve the constant sawing and hammering. I texted Grayson to let him know.

He wrote me back with lots of smiley faces, which made me smile again. Then he texted that he was working on a follow-up story to the news article on Vivian's death, which had run in today's edition. The new story was going to focus on quotes from people who knew Vivian and how her murder affected the community. He asked if I wanted to go with him to interview a former client of Vivian's, Jessica Morton, who'd reached out to the paper on Facebook. He'd set up a visit with her at her house in about an hour. He gave me the address.

I quickly accepted over text, then swung my legs out of the bed. Fitz gave me a disappointed look.

"Sorry, buddy. I've got to meet up with Grayson." I reached over to tickle him under his furry chin.

After I'd gotten ready and grabbed something to eat, I hurried out to my car. But before I could get there, I spotted Zelda marching up the walk, clipboard in hand.

I groaned. I'd forgotten Zelda had wanted a tour of the construction zone that morning. I quickly texted Grayson that I'd be waylaid for an additional fifteen minutes. I hoped the fifteen minutes weren't wishful thinking.

Zelda was clearly wearing what I'd catalogued as her "official HOA business" outfit of sensible shoes, reading glasses on a chain, and a pen behind her ear. She checked her watch as she approached.

"I said I'd be by," she stated with satisfaction. "I'm a woman of my word."

"Of course you are," I said. "Come on in. I've got about fifteen minutes before I need to meet up with Grayson, if that's okay?"

"That's all I need," she said with a sniff.

"Would you like a cup of coffee?"

Zelda shook her head. "I'm here in an official capacity, so no. Especially if we're in a time crunch."

Fitz came trotting up to say hi. He looked slightly flummoxed that I was back inside after having clearly left the house, but pleased that I'd turned around. Zelda softened, looking a little less official as she bent to love on the cat for a minute. "How's Mr. Fitz handling the construction?" she asked gruffly.

"He's not crazy about the noise. He'd probably tell us that his naps have declined in quality and probably quantity, too. But you know Fitz. The workmen all love him, and he's been curious to see what's been going on with the addition."

Zelda bobbed her head. "As I am. Well, let's get on with it." She peered at her clipboard, which appeared to have a laminated checklist with specific line items. Then she started moving through the cottage with the focus of a building inspector and the suspicion of a detective during an interrogation.

I was both surprised and impressed by the inspection. Somehow, I'd thought Zelda was just wanting to be nosy and see how the construction was coming. But she was acting as if she were a government official instead of merely a homeowner association president. She made sure the window placement compared with the approved plans of the HOA architectural board. She asked which walls were load-bearing. She checked the ceiling height in the additions. Then she ensured the electrical outlet placement followed code ("Every twelve feet. I'm counting.")

Zelda was intense and focused throughout the entire inspection, treating the cottage addition with great seriousness. She frowned at a tarp. "That could count as an unauthorized temporary structure." She scowled at the recycling bin that was visible from the street during the construction. "Section four, paragraph seven," she muttered under her breath. She jotted down notes about the tarp and bin, handing them to me. "I'll note this as 'observed, but not cited.' Consider it a warning."

I thanked her with the appropriate amount of gravity.

Zelda and I headed to the door. She studied me for a moment. "You look tired. More tired than your construction warrants, I think."

"Well, it's been a challenging few days."

Zelda narrowed her eyes. "I heard about the wedding planner. Terrible business." Then she shifted gears. "Your construction is on schedule?"

"That's what I understand."

Zelda leaned in. "You'll need to stay on top of them. Or, if you need someone to put pressure on the workers, let me know. I'll handle it."

With that, Zelda left with the same purposeful stride she'd arrived with. I climbed into my car, smiling at the thought of Zelda being our enforcer.

When I arrived at Jessica's house, Grayson had just pulled in. Jessica's house was small but well-maintained, with a perfectly centered fall wreath on her front door. The realtor had probably listed it as a starter home. When Grayson knocked at the door, a woman in her late-twenties appeared. She was dressed casually but neatly in jeans and a nice sweater, the kind of outfit that took effort to look effortless. She wore a locket and a charm bracelet that jingled softly as she opened the door. She smoothed down her sweater and touched her locket with one hand, almost for reassurance.

"You must be Grayson Phillips. And Ann, I've seen you at the library."

I nodded. No wonder she'd looked familiar to me. "Good to see you."

"Please, come inside."

Jessica's living room was immaculate, with magazines perfectly fanned out on a coffee table. The coasters were exactly centered, and there was no dust to be seen. There was a wedding photo on a shelf of Jessica in white alongside a smiling husband. They looked happy, like people whose big day had gone according to plan. An open laptop sat on a desk, with a headset nearby. There was no sign of any clutter.

She motioned for us to take a seat, and we settled into armchairs. Grayson said, "Thanks again for meeting with us. As I'd mentioned, I was looking for former clients and colleagues of Vivian's to get a well-sourced story on her."

Jessica nodded. "That's so important. Getting the full picture."

"So, Vivian planned your own wedding, I understand?" Grayson asked.

"That's right. It was a couple of years ago now." She gave a short laugh. "It's kind of strange, isn't it? I mean, talking about someone after they're gone. You want to be honest, but you also don't want to speak ill of the dead. Oh, I forgot to ask if you wanted anything to drink. A glass of water? Coffee?"

Grayson and I shook our heads. Grayson said, "I totally understand about not wanting to say anything bad about someone who's passed. Does that mean you had a tough experience with Vivian when you were planning your wedding?"

Jessica's expression shifted. "Unfortunately, our wedding wasn't exactly what we'd planned. The flowers were wrong, totally wrong. They were the wrong color. Our wedding cake was three hours late." She gave another short laugh, this one harsher. "Then there was an argument between Vivian and our photographer that lasted half the reception."

She spoke calmly, as if she'd told the story many times. And maybe she had. She was clearly very disappointed in the wedding's outcome.

Grayson glanced over at me as if he needed me to step in. I said, "That must have been so hard. So much planning goes into weddings and to have it all fall apart on your big day must have really hurt."

Jessica nodded, apparently glad I understood. "Exactly. I had Pinterest boards for color swatches. I had mood boards. I knew exactly what I wanted down to the ribbon on the programs." Her gaze went distant for a moment. "I mean, the flowers were supposed to be blush pink. I wanted them soft, romantic, and elegant. But they were neon fuchsia, like something from a gas station bouquet. I can still picture them in my mind. It's like every detail of that day is very clear to me." She gave a short laugh, but there was no humor in it.

Grayson tapped his pen on his notebook. "I'm sure it is. I'm sorry you had such a bad experience with Vivian."

"I can still picture everything perfectly. Every detail of that day is very clear to me. I mean, the wrong flowers, the missing cake, and Vivian arguing with the photographer while my grandma sat there waiting to give her toast. It was a nightmare. You don't forget a day like that."

We nodded our heads sympathetically.

"And, again, I'm sorry to bring this up. Vivian is dead, after all. But I couldn't stand by without letting you know the full story on Vivian. Maybe it'll resonate with other brides. We all want everything to be perfect on our big day, you know? When it falls through, it can really hurt." She sighed. "And people don't always understand how *much* it can hurt. Except the police, I guess. Chief Edison came by to speak to me yesterday."

"Did he?" asked Grayson slowly. "How did Burton know about your experience with Vivian?"

"He didn't say, but I'm assuming it's because of the negative reviews I left for her online." Jessica shook her head. "I couldn't let other brides stumble into the same situation with Vivian without giving them a heads-up." She gave a bitter laugh. "Do you know, Vivian called me up after I wrote the reviews, demanding I retract them. Can you believe it? She said it was libel. Nope. It was just the truth. Of course I kept them up."

"Were you able to help out Chief Edison?"

Jessica said, "Not really. He apparently thought I might be a suspect. I told him he must not have realized how many people Vivian had upset in this town. But unfortunately for me, I didn't have an alibi. I was here working at home." She gestured to the laptop and headset. "I do customer service work remotely. If I'd known I needed an alibi, I'd have gotten one."

I said, "You must be feeling so bitter about what happened with your wedding. Planners aren't cheap, and then to have a disaster happen makes it so much worse."

"Honestly, it made me feel sorry for Vivian in some ways. Well, I felt sorry for myself, first of all. But then I started thinking about Vivian. She cared so much about having everything be perfect and about having 'the best' of everything. But she never, ever apologized to me when everything at my wedding fell apart."

Grayson shook his head. "That's awful. And totally unprofessional, considering Vivian was in charge of making sure everything went according to plan."

"I think Vivian couldn't even admit mistakes to herself. Apologizing would mean admitting she failed. That's a really sad way to live." She gave a small smile. "I've been working hard to move forward. I only revisit this when I want to give cautionary tales to other brides. That's why I think it's important to have a well-balanced account of Vivian's life."

Jessica was showing a lot more grace to Vivian than I thought I'd be able to in the same situation.

Grayson said, "I bet having a wedding disaster can put a lot of stress on both the bride and groom. That's a rough way to start out a marriage. How did you and your husband get through it?"

Jessica said slowly, "It was hard. Really hard, actually. We're still working through things. I've had to learn that your wedding day isn't your marriage. The day was a disaster, but the marriage itself is all that matters."

I looked over at the wedding photo again. The couple looked happy in the picture. Genuinely happy. Jessica's smile reached her eyes. Her husband had his arm around her waist like he never wanted to let go. Maybe it was a photo shoot before all the chaos of the wedding, or maybe they'd been able to fake it for the camera.

Grayson said, "Have you heard of other clients who had issues with Vivian? Just curious."

"Oh, definitely. That big wedding Vivian always used to brag about? The one she planned in Charlotte before moving here? Anyway, I've heard it was a nightmare, too. And I think the florist here has had a lot of issues with Vivian."

"Sarah Chen?" I asked.

"I don't know her personally, but I've heard Vivian was hard on all the local vendors, including Sarah. She thought they weren't up to her standards."

Grayson asked, "Did Vivian line you up with local vendors for your wedding?"

"No, she was always really derogatory when she talked about them. We ended up using businesses in Asheville and Charlotte. Vivian set it all up, of course."

Grayson said, "Do you have any idea who might have wanted to harm Vivian?"

"Unfortunately, that's probably plenty of people. Her ex-husband, for one. Have you spoken to Tom yet?"

"Not yet. He's on my list though," said Grayson.

Jessica lowered her voice as if sharing something delicate. "I've heard their divorce was brutal. Really bitter." She paused. "I'm not sure how to say this without sounding like I'm accusing anyone, but I've heard Tom's been acting strange lately. Someone told me he was at the post office last week practically losing it over a package. It was like he'd snapped. I keep hearing he's on edge lately. I was wondering if it was financial stress from the divorce."

"What's he like?" I asked.

"Well, not like that. Not usually, anyway. And, look, I'm not saying he did anything. But I know ex-husbands might be the kind of people cops would be looking at. They're the obvious suspects, right?"

Jessica continued after a moment. "There's that other wedding planner, too. Patricia something? Maybe Patricia Holbrook. I heard Vivian stole a lot of her business. She had twenty years of building a reputation, and suddenly everyone wanted the fancy wedding planner from the big city. I'd think that would create a lot of resentment."

Grayson asked Jessica a few more questions, mostly general questions for background on Vivian, as if his interest was solely in an article. Then we stood to leave.

We stood for a couple of minutes at our cars. The sun was warm, but I felt a small chill.

Grayson said quietly, "Wow. It sounds like Vivian really butchered her wedding."

"Which is so odd. We could both tell Vivian was a total perfectionist. Perfectionists aren't usually the kinds of people who screw things up, at least not to that degree."

Grayson said, "It sounded like Jessica was a lot more forgiving than a lot of people would be."

"How did you get her name again? Did you say it was from Facebook or something?"

Grayson nodded. "That's right. She'd made a comment on the newspaper's post on Vivian's death. She wanted to talk with the paper about Vivian. I had no idea she was going to do a hatchet job on her. I'd originally wondered if she could maybe point us to other suspects."

"Which she did, actually. Vivian's ex-husband and that other wedding planner. I know Patricia from the library. She attends book club there."

"Gotcha." Grayson looked at his watch and made a face. He leaned over to give me a peck on the cheek. "Sorry, but I've got to run. I've got a staff meeting in a few minutes. Are you working today?"

"Yes, I'm going to head over there now. Well, after I grab Fitz. But I'll be off by mid-afternoon . . . I'm not closing up today."

Grayson said, "I'll check in with you later, then."

We headed our separate ways. I dropped back by the house and collected Fitz before driving over to the library.

Chapter Seven

At the library, Fitz stretched as he came out of his carrier, his intelligent green eyes surveying the area. When he saw the toddler storytime in the children's section, which this time appeared to be blissfully noisemaker-free, he bounded over.

"I've never seen a cat who wants to hang out with toddlers," said a dry voice behind me. "Don't they pull his tail?"

I turned to see Patricia Holbrook there. I was marveling at the fact she materialized shortly after Jessica had mentioned her as a potential suspect when I realized it was time for her monthly book club meeting. From what I remembered, Patricia actually led the meetings.

"No, the moms tend to make sure the kids are really gentle," I said. "And, of course, Fitz can easily bound away if everything gets to be too much. Although it never seems to." I looked at the book she was holding.

"*The Thursday Murder Club.*" Patricia held it up. "Have you read it?"

"It's on my list. What's it about?"

Patricia said, "Four retirees in a retirement home who investigate cold cases. It's very cozy and fun. Although I have to admit, murder seems less cozy and fun when it's happening in your own town." She gave me a meaningful look.

"I'm sorry about Vivian," I said carefully. "I know you were colleagues." More like competitors, if Jessica was to be believed, but I didn't mention that.

Patricia gave me a smile. "Yes, it's very hard. Disturbing. The poor woman." Then she shifted gears smoothly, clearly more comfortable discussing weddings than murder. "So you're getting married in October, aren't you? That's a lovely time of year. The light is gorgeous for photographs."

"That's what we're hoping for."

She waited a few beats before saying, "And now you're without your wedding planner. That's quite a quandary. Are you still looking for someone? Or at least some coordination help?" Her tone was brisk, but not pushy.

"We're figuring it out. Grayson and I are pretty low-key."

Patricia took out a small leather notebook. "Low-key is fine. But low-key still needs someone to make sure the caterer shows up."

"I've got a few weeks." I meant it to sound like I had plenty of time, but it came out sounding like a pittance.

Patricia nodded. "I felt so sorry for you and Grayson when I heard the news. You don't want to grapple with all the minutia for planning when you're both working." She reached into her purse and pulled out a business card. "I hope you don't think I'm really tacky for doing this. Honestly, I was thinking about you, not thinking about drumming up business."

I opened my mouth to tell her I wasn't interested in getting another planner when she continued. "What's your guest count looking like? And I always like to ask early if there are any family considerations I should know about. Divorced parents who can't sit together, that sort of thing?"

"Actually, it's pretty simple on my end," I said carefully. "There are no family complications."

Patricia had pulled out a pen and a small notebook. "That's refreshing. So your parents are still together?"

"It's just me." I kept my voice light. I'd had years of practice with this conversation. "My mother passed away when I was a child. I never knew my father. My great-aunt raised me, but she's been gone for a while now."

To her credit, Patricia didn't do the dramatic sympathy routine with the head tilt and the "oh, you poor thing" that many people did. She simply nodded and made a note.

"So no corsages for the mother of the bride, no boutonniere for the father of the bride. That simplifies the flower order, of course." She looked up. "Who's walking you down the aisle? Or are you doing the modern thing and walking yourself?"

"I'm going to ask Wilson. He's my director here at the library."

Patricia's eyebrows rose slightly. "Wilson Trent? Really?"

"He's been good to me. And he saved my life recently, so it seems fitting."

"Well." Patricia closed her notebook. "That's rather lovely, actually. Not traditional, but meaningful. That's what matters."

I appreciated that she didn't dwell on it. Some people wanted the entire story and would ask how I lost my mom or what it had been like growing up without parents. They might have asked if I was sad my mother wouldn't see my wedding. But Patricia filed the information away and kept going. Maybe it was something about very practical people. They didn't need you to perform your grief for them. But there was still the fact that Grayson and I wanted to take over the planning ourselves.

I took the card, putting it in the pocket of my black slacks. "Thanks, Patricia. I'll keep this handy, in case I need to give you a call. But Grayson and I were thinking about handling the rest of the details ourselves. If that plan doesn't work out, I'll reach out to you, for sure."

Patricia's face fell for a moment before she could resume her usual, professional countenance. "No worries! I'm here if you need me. I have a lot of experience with wedding planning, all of it here in Whitby."

I could tell from her expression that she seemed to think Vivian paled in comparison. "That's wonderful, Patricia. You must really know all the vendors and venues here."

"I do," said Patricia eagerly. She hesitated, then added, "I'm not going to say Vivian didn't do a good job. It's just that she hadn't been in town as long as I have. And although she quickly integrated into the market here, she didn't have good business relationships with the vendors."

I said, "I heard she could be difficult to work with."

"That's something of an understatement," said Patricia, some bitterness underneath her determinedly professional tone. "And her manner when she arrived rubbed some people the wrong way. She moved here from Charlotte several years ago and was very condescending about the venues Whitby offers. Vivian acted as if she was really slumming, just living here. And she pushed against anyone wanting something very simple. Did you notice that?"

I nodded. "She tended to want the best for her clients. At least, that was my take on it."

"Exactly," said Patricia eagerly. "But if someone wants a basic wedding, they should get a basic wedding. Not everything has to be sophisticated, expensive, and elevated. And she certainly didn't understand the importance of family and traditions here, and the need people have to make a special day very personal. Maybe clients wanted to use their grandmother's china at the wedding reception, for example. Vivian wouldn't permit something like that."

"Did you lose much business to Vivian?"

"Oh, gracious, yes," said Patricia. "Several large weddings, an anniversary celebration, and other events. But I have to hand it to her. She was both very impressive and very persuasive." She gave me a sad smile. "I lost your business, too."

It was true. Vivian had come on like a force of nature. At the time she pitched her wedding planning services to me, I was simply eager to hand it all over and go the route of least resistance. I didn't even consider calling to interview other planners. "I'm sorry about that," I said genuinely.

Patricia waved her hand as if to dismiss my apology. "It's business, isn't it? Believe me, I understand. And Vivian came across very well. She had all these big weddings on her resume. The Morrison wedding at the Biltmore Estate, and things like that." She sighed. "But it hurt, all the same. Especially when Vivian was bad-mouthing me around town."

"Was she? I had no idea."

Patricia nodded. "She told everyone my weddings were old-fashioned or quaint. That my work wasn't the aesthetic clients would want for their weddings."

I was about to ask more about this when I was suddenly interrupted by none other than Mrs. Sullivan, my two-factor patron. "Ann, I need you to witness this."

I gave Patricia an apologetic look. I thought Patricia might need to move on to her book club meeting, but a quick glance at the wall clock told me she had arrived at the library twenty minutes early, probably hoping to talk with me about wedding planning services before book club started.

"Is it your bank app again?" I asked Mrs. Sullivan.

"It is. This will only take a moment." She set her tablet on the desk with the air of a prosecutor presenting evidence. "Watch this."

She navigated to the bank login, entered her credentials, then waited.

The two-factor authentication prompt appeared. Mrs. Sullivan's phone buzzed with the code.

"Now look carefully."

Mrs. Sullivan typed in the code deliberately and correctly. With the focus of someone defusing a bomb.

The screen refreshed. *Code expired. Please try again.*

"You see?" Mrs. Sullivan turned to me triumphantly. "It's not a user error. The system is fundamentally flawed. And it's not the first time, as I've been telling you. Look at these pictures I took at home."

She held up her phone to show me pictures of an actual stopwatch at various times. "All the attempts were well within a thirty-second window."

I wasn't entirely sure how to troubleshoot this one. Mrs. Sullivan had apparently done everything right. I'd watched her enter the code myself. It was within the time window.

"May I see your phone for a moment?" I asked.

She handed it over with the air of someone who'd been vindicated and was now allowing the expert to verify her findings.

I opened her text messages. The problem was staring back at me in a neat little column. Her texts from the bank read like a numerical archaeological dig:

Your verification code is 847291. Do not share this number! Your verification code is 336518. Do not share this number! Your verification code is 571034. Do not share this number!

And so on.

"Mrs. Sullivan, which code did you enter just now?"

"The one they sent me, of course. I can still remember it. 448127."

I checked the text messages. It was the number on the very top of the heap of texts from the bank.

"That's the first code they sent you. It could be from days ago."

Mrs. Sullivan squinted at the screen. "But it's right there at the top."

"Text messages put the newest ones on the bottom. The one at the top is the oldest one."

There was a long pause. I saw Patricia trying to hide a smile.

Mrs. Sullivan's expression cycled through disbelief, indignation, then something that might have qualified as embarrassment on anyone else's face. On Mrs. Sullivan, however, it looked more like she was reconsidering her opinion of the entire telecommunications industry.

"That's a ridiculous system," she said finally. "Newest at the bottom. Who decided that?"

"I'm not sure, but I don't disagree with you."

She scowled. "It's completely counterintuitive. The newest message should be right at the top where you can see it. Not buried at the bottom where you have to scroll."

"You're not wrong."

Mrs. Sullivan watched as I cleared out the old messages, leaving only the most recent code. Then I handed the phone back to her. "I'm writing a letter to someone about this. Recent messages on the top. It's common sense."

She tried the login again on her tablet with the correct code. The screen welcomed her to her account. She put her phone down.

"There," I said. "You're all set."

Mrs. Sullivan gathered up her devices with her dignity intact. "Thank you, Ann. Though I maintain the system is fundamentally hostile to users of a certain generation."

"You may be right about that."

She marched off toward the computer area, and I turned back to Patricia, who'd watched the entire exchange with amusement. She said, "And once again, a librarian saves the day."

I gave a mock bow. "I do what I can."

"What were we talking about?" asked Patricia. "I've somehow lost track."

Chapter Eight

"We were talking about the big events Vivian had done. The Morrison wedding at the Biltmore Estate, for one. Vivian talked about it constantly."

Patricia's laugh was sharp. "Of course she did. Did she mention that her big society wedding was a total catastrophe?"

My eyebrows rose. "No. What happened?"

"Everything that could go wrong, went wrong. The arbor collapsed outright during the vows. It toppled right over. The monogrammed napkins had the wrong initials, which might have been forgivable if the initials hadn't spelled out a rude word. The fog machine for the first dance was set too high, and the wedding video is very cloudy in response."

"Goodness," I said mildly.

But the litany of issues at the famed Morrison wedding continued. "Vivian positioned the confetti cannon for the exit wrong and it fired directly into the grandmother of the bride. The doves refused to fly during the release. They huddled there on the lawn while the photographer tried to get the shot." There was a certain vindictive glee in Patricia's voice.

"Well, that's a real mess," I said. Which was an obvious understatement.

A harried-looking woman approached with a stack of books and a toddler attached to her leg.

"Excuse me. I'm so sorry to interrupt. Do you have any books about getting toddlers to sleep? I mean, ones that actually work? Because I've tried everything and nothing seems to help. I haven't slept in three days, and I'm starting to hallucinate."

Her toddler gave me a gleeful grin.

"Let me show you what we have. Patricia, if you could give me a moment?"

I guided the woman to the parenting section, showed her three books with completely different approaches. I returned to find Patricia examining her nails with barely concealed irritation. "Sorry about that."

"No, no. Public servant. I understand." Patricia's tone suggested she didn't entirely.

"You were talking about the Morrison wedding at the Biltmore Estate. How poorly it went," I said helpfully.

"Right. Anyway, her reputation in Charlotte was completely annihilated after that, which is why she moved here."

I frowned. "I thought it had to do with following her husband here. Or her husband at the time. I know they're divorced now."

Patricia waved her hand in the air with a dismissive gesture. "That was just a cover. Vivian needed a fresh market, one that wasn't aware of her high-profile failure. Tom followed along. When their marriage fell apart, they both stayed here. Vivian reinvented herself as the sophisticate bringing city elegance to small-town charm."

"Running away from a professional failure."

"A *massive* professional failure," said Patricia with satisfaction in her voice. "What's more, she tore down everyone around her. If she made local vendors or venues look incompetent, no one would question whether *she* was competent."

I nodded. "It sounds like her arrival really affected your business."

Patricia gave a short laugh. "Everyone's struggling these days. Weddings are getting smaller and budgets are tighter."

"But you're managing?"

"I'm fine," said Patricia. "I've been doing this for twenty-two years. I have loyal clients and families who appreciate tradition over trends." She lifted her chin. "Vivian was a blip on the radar. An annoying blip, but temporary."

"I'm sure others probably found Vivian difficult, too."

Patricia leaned in. "Have you spoken to Jasper Webb? The caterer?"

I kept my expression neutral. "About Vivian?"

"I won't be surprised if the police are looking at him. I've worked with Jasper on events for years. Don't get me wrong; he's a real sweetheart. But Vivian pushed him too far."

I asked, "Was there a specific incident? Or did she just push him in general?"

"Both. About six weeks ago, I was coordinating a rehearsal dinner. It was the Parker-Collins wedding. Vivian was handling the wedding itself the next day. She cornered Jasper in the kitchen and laid into him about his menu. She called his grandmother's biscuit recipe 'pedestrian.'"

I winced. Jasper was very proud of those biscuits. I was still hoping I could sample them later on.

Patricia continued. "Then Vivian said his barbeque was fine for a church picnic, but not a sophisticated event."

"That sounds like Vivian. But Jasper seems like the kind of person who'd let it roll off him. At least, from what I've seen."

"That's what I thought, too," said Patricia. "He's a pretty laid-back guy. But I was getting napkins from the back hallway, and I could hear them arguing. Jasper was saying that he'd been catering for fifteen years and knew what he was doing. Vivian said she'd stop recommending him to clients if he didn't do a better job with what he offered."

She paused for effect. "Then Jasper said, and I remember this clearly, that she should find another caterer. That he was done letting her treat his kitchen like it was hers."

We were quiet for a few moments. Then Patricia said, "I'm not saying Jasper did anything. I'm just saying Vivian threatened his business. He depends on wedding referrals. And she was at his farmhouse when she died, after all."

"Have you told Burton this?"

Patricia shrugged. "Not yet. I only remembered it last night. I'll give him a call. He does need someone else to look at besides me. I'm sure he thinks I'm a logical suspect, since Vivian and I were competitors, of a sort. But competition is healthy. I certainly didn't wish Vivian any harm."

Then she suddenly changed course again. "Look, Ann. I know this is a difficult time, but I want to be direct with you.

Your wedding is in a few weeks, your caterer's business is a crime scene, and your planner is dead. You have my business card. Believe me, I have the ability to step in and handle everything. I can coordinate with your vendors, organize your venue, and make sure your day goes smoothly."

I shook my head. "The venue is at my house."

Patricia raised an eyebrow. "Actually, I know where you live. I've seen you out gardening when I've driven by. Aren't they doing construction there right now?"

"They're finishing up the sunroom."

There must have been some uncertainty in my voice because Patricia suddenly gave a rather triumphant smile. "Is that what they're saying? Because nothing, nothing with contractors ever runs on time. It just never does. You could be saying your vows, and they could be hammering and drilling feet away, drowning them all out with construction racket."

She'd finally hit a sore spot. I had a latent fear about our big day.

Patricia said, "I can coordinate them, too. I know how to keep on those guys, making sure they stay on task. Or, if all else fails, I have the contacts to arrange a last-minute substitute venue. I've been doing this for twenty-two years. I know every backup option in this county."

Part of me would have felt relieved at the thought of handing it off and letting Patricia handle everything. But another part of me thought this was the opportunity to take the reins and do everything the way Grayson and I originally wanted it to be done.

"I appreciate the offer," I said. "Really. But I think Grayson and I need to figure this all out." Besides, Zelda had already offered to be our construction enforcer. And she was intimidating.

Patricia's smile tightened. "Of course. Just call me whenever you're ready. I hope your wedding is everything you want it to be. Some of us planners actually do care about that." Patricia glanced at her watch. "I should head to the community room. Book club is getting ready to start now."

"Of course. Thanks for talking with me, Patricia."

"Anytime." Patricia paused, and something flickered across her face. I couldn't tell if it was vulnerability or calculation. "I know people will be talking about Vivian and who might have wanted to hurt her. I hope they'll remember I've been part of this community for over two decades. That has to count for something."

Before I could respond, she hurried toward the community room, her low heels clicking against the floor.

Chapter Nine

"Ann?"

I turned to find Mona, Luna's mom and Wilson's fiancée, approaching. Her knitting bag was slung over one shoulder, and she had a hopeful expression on her face.

"Heading to book club?" I asked.

"In a minute." She glanced toward the community room. "I wanted to catch you first. Was that Patricia Holbrook you were talking to?"

"That's right. She's in your book club, isn't she?"

Mona nodded. "She seems lovely. Very put-together." She hesitated, fidgeting with the strap of her knitting bag. "Actually, I wanted to ask you something. Wilson and I are getting a bit overwhelmed with our wedding planning. I'm sure you must understand. Wilson keeps making spreadsheets, but spreadsheets aren't the same as someone who actually knows what they're doing."

I had the feeling I knew where this was going.

"Luna mentioned Patricia does wedding planning," Mona continued. "It's a topic that hasn't come up during our book club meetings. We do stay pretty focused on the books we're reading. Anyway, Luna said Patricia does traditional weddings. Everything very family-focused, which sounds exactly like what we want. It would be wonderful to have someone to help us pull it all together." Mona gave me a warm smile. "Do you think Patricia might be a good choice? I'd really value your opinion."

There it was. I wasn't sure I could answer honestly without explaining I was mentally cataloging Patricia as a murder suspect.

"I think . . . " I started, then stopped. What did I think? Patricia was definitely experienced and seemed to know everything about vendors and venues. She obviously knew Whitby and its traditions. But I also thought she could have had a vendetta against my former wedding planner, who was now dead.

"I think you should talk to another planner first. I think there's one other one in town now. Patricia does have a lot of experience, and she obviously cares about making weddings personal. But she does make a pretty strong sales pitch. Maybe talk to her if you're not as happy with the other local planner. You want someone you really connect with."

Mona tilted her head slightly. "That's very diplomatic of you, Ann. And you're right. It's a big decision, and I shouldn't just jump at the first option. I'm not a fan of hard sells, either." Mona added, "I better go in there before they start without me. We're discussing *The Thursday Murder Club*. I have opinions about it," she said with a laugh. She squeezed my arm. "Thanks, Ann. You're always so thoughtful."

The rest of the day passed by in the usual rhythm. Patrons came and went. Fitz happily napped in various sunny spots in the library.

Later, back home at the cottage, Grayson was already there when I arrived and had put our Mexican takeout on plates. Fitz quickly bounded up to say hi to him.

Grayson cuddled him for a minute before smiling up at me. "How is everything going?"

"Busy day, but it was a good one. How about you? Were you still working on the story about Vivian?"

"I'm not sure what I was working on is actually going to make it into an article. It was mostly background stuff. Or maybe just context. Or, possibly, I spent a lot of time going down a rabbit hole on the internet. You know how that goes."

We sat down at the table and started eating. "What kind of rabbit hole did you fall down?"

"That Morrison wedding that Vivian was so proud of. The one that was held at the Biltmore Estate."

I raised my eyebrows. "Oh wow. I heard a bunch about that today, myself. I had a long conversation with Patricia Holbrook, a wedding planner. What did you read?"

"The event was semi-documented. There was a forum where vendors for the event were complaining about Vivian. At least, that's how it started. Then Vivian's former clients hopped on the forum and started bashing how Vivian had handled their events."

I said, "Sounds like a bunch of angry brides."

"Brides for sure, but Vivian's services also extended to anniversary parties, corporate events, and that sort of thing. She was really more of an *event* planner in Charlotte. Of course, Whitby is a lot smaller, so it's mostly just weddings."

I said, "Vivian was pretty bold to brag about doing the Morrison wedding when anyone could find out online how poorly it went."

"True. But honestly, how much digging do people do when they're hiring a wedding planner? You and I didn't check into Vivian's background."

I gave him a rueful smile. "You're right. We were glad not to have all that planning to do by ourselves. At least initially."

"And I don't think we're the only ones. From what I saw, Vivian's business really went downhill in Charlotte, which precipitated the move here. I'm not even sure Vivian actually followed her husband down here; I think it might have been the other way around," said Grayson.

"Which isn't what Vivian said. I'd gotten the impression she'd graciously moved here because Tom had a job offer."

"I think Vivian might have been very good at covering up unwanted truths. I looked up her ex-husband, Tom Cross. He doesn't seem to have a job right now. His LinkedIn profile has him listed as actively looking."

I said, "So Vivian needed to get out of Charlotte where her business was going rapidly downhill. Her husband left his own job to follow her to Whitby. But now, Vivian is dead, and he's still looking for work."

"That's what it looks like." Grayson took a bite of his enchilada, chewing thoughtfully. "It's kind of strange he'd have divorced Vivian, isn't it? Considering she was the only one generating income."

"Maybe it's a sign of how bad things were in their marriage. Or maybe Vivian was the one who ended things."

Grayson nodded. "Okay, so Tom's definitely a suspect, mainly because spouses or ex-spouses are always high on the list. We have Jessica Morton, who's wedding was destroyed by Vivian."

"Right. She did reach out to the newspaper to complain about how Vivian mangled her wedding. There's that."

"True," said Grayson. "She might not have been as over the wedding disaster as she sounded. Then we have Jasper, I guess. After all, they weren't getting along with each other. Plus, Vivian was found dead at his business."

I nodded, mouth full of a taco.

Grayson continued. "Sarah Chen wasn't crazy about Vivian, either, so I suppose she's also a suspect."

"Sadly. And I do really like Sarah. But she does have motive. And, like I mentioned, I spoke with Patricia Holbrook at the library today. She's another suspect for our list."

Grayson said, "Right, she's a wedding planner. Actually, isn't Patricia the *only* other wedding planner in Whitby?"

"There's one other, but I'm not completely sure she does it full-time. Patricia wasn't especially happy when Vivian moved in from Charlotte and started stealing all her business away from her."

"No, I'd imagine not. Did Patricia offer to plan our wedding for us?"

I rolled my eyes. "Oh, definitely. She was really pitching me. I managed to put her off, though. Going back to the suspects, none of them have solid alibis."

"Classic," said Grayson. "What's your gut saying right now?"

"My gut's pretty confused. But sadly, I'm leaning toward Jasper. Maybe his 'discovering Vivian's body' with me was a total set-up to make him look innocent. I really like him, but he was definitely unhappy with Vivian."

We ate in comfortable silence for a few minutes. Grayson said, "So, going back to Patricia. You said you could stall her when she pushed to be our planner. We're going to manage our own planning at this point?"

"Only if that's okay with you. Sorry, I should have asked you about it. But Patricia was being so bossy. She kept saying she could step in and handle everything, even keeping the contractors on-task."

Grayson snorted. "That would be a job in itself."

"Exactly. And I'm not saying it didn't sound like a big relief, in some ways. But I'm not sure I want someone else handling it at this point. Vivian was pushing us away from the wedding we wanted and now we have the chance to get what we actually want."

Grayson nodded. "You know, I've been thinking about all those elevated options Vivian kept pushing. None of them felt like us." He reached across the table for my hand. "What if we keep it simple? What if we just went with the cottage garden, family and friends, and Jasper's Southern cooking?"

"It sounds a lot more like what we wanted at the beginning of the planning process." Then I smiled. "Hey, I almost forgot to tell you about Zelda's inspection this morning."

"Wow, that had totally slipped my mind."

I laughed. "You'd probably repressed the memory. She had a laminated checklist, Grayson. Laminated."

"Of course she did."

I added, "She counted the electrical outlets. Apparently, code requires them every twelve feet. Zelda seemed very disappointed when everything checked out."

"No violations, then?"

I said, "Nothing really specific to the construction. But she was unhappy about a tarp and our recycling bin. Fortunately, she must have been in a good mood this morning. She gave me a formal warning, telling me the violations were observed, but not cited." I shook my head. "She treated our cottage addition like a federal investigation. Meanwhile, I'm trying to figure out who killed our wedding planner, and Zelda's measuring the ceiling height with a tape measure she brought from home."

"At least she's thorough."

I nodded. "She also offered to boss around our construction team in case they started slipping off schedule."

Grayson raised an eyebrow. "Okay. So basically like a hired gun."

"I know. I'm not sure whether to be touched or terrified."

Grayson laughed and reached for another chip to dip into our queso. We finished our meal talking about much easier topics, like a movie he wanted to see, a book I'd been meaning to read, and how relieved Fitz would be when the construction chaos had wrapped up.

Later, after Grayson had gone home, I fell asleep thinking about garden flowers, a sunny day, and Grayson's hand in mine.

Chapter Ten

The next morning was more leisurely since I wasn't on the schedule at the library. The construction crew seemed like they were getting a later start, too.

I'd just fed Fitz and was filling up a mug with coffee when I saw a colorful car consumed by bumper stickers pull up outside. I smiled. Luna. I wasn't sure what she was doing at my house, but she always had the ability to entertain me.

Before she'd had the chance to knock, I pulled open the door. "Well, hello there!" said Luna, beaming at me.

Fitz, having finished his breakfast, bounded over to rub against Luna's legs. She crooned to him as she walked in.

"Want some coffee?" I asked.

"See, this is what I love about you, Ann. You're totally unflappable. Someone comes to your door unexpectedly while you're in your pjs? Not a problem for you. Yes, I'd love some coffee."

Luna settled at the kitchen table with Fitz in her lap. The two of them appeared to be having a lovefest as I brought the coffee back to her.

Luna waved a brown bag at me. "I did bring some pastries from Keep Grounded with me. As sort of an apology for dropping by."

I pulled out some napkins, and we sat there, eating pastries, drinking coffee, and chitchatting.

Luna polished off her pastry and said, "You're probably wondering why I'm here but are too polite to ask. When I realized we both had the day off from the library, I thought I'd come by and see how the new addition and the rest of the construction was coming along." She looked around her, frowning. "Where are those construction guys, by the way? Shouldn't they be here hammering and whatnot?"

"Don't jinx us. It's nice and quiet right now. But I'm sure they'll be along soon. I'm hoping most of the work will be done before the wedding. At least, most of the really loud part of the work."

I took Luna on a little tour, starting with the new sunroom. It felt nice to show off what had been accomplished. And it felt very different from the tour I'd given laser-focused Zelda yesterday morning. We walked through plastic sheeting into the new construction.

"Hey, this is going to be really great. Looks like there are going to be tons of sunbeams for Fitz. But then, I guess that's the point of a sunroom."

Fitz, who'd followed us, quickly claimed a sunny spot on the exposed subflooring.

I took her through to see the small additional bedroom we'd opted for. Then we walked into an area that was going to serve as a sort of library/den. This was the part that really got Luna's attention. The wall framing showed where the built-in bookcases would go.

"Combined book collections," said Luna. "That's serious commitment."

"We still have to negotiate shelf space," I said with a laugh.

"You two have really figured it all out, haven't you? The whole making two lives fit together thing."

I said after a moment, "Well, it's a work in progress. Sort of like the construction." I paused. She seemed a little morose, which was an unusual emotion for Luna. I didn't want to pry, but I also wondered if Luna's visit was for more than just seeing the construction. "Is everything okay with you and Jeremy?"

Luna sighed. "Let's get some more coffee."

We settled in the kitchen with our mugs. Luna took a deep breath. "Jeremy got a job offer."

"He's already got a job," I said with a frown. "Was he looking for something else?"

"No. A recruiter at this company reached out to him. I guess they were looking for an IT person with his skill-set and saw his LinkedIn or something. Anyway, the problem is that this offer is in Charlotte."

I winced. Charlotte was a couple of hours away. "Is it a remote job?"

"Nope. In person. And it has significantly better pay." Luna sighed. "He's excited, Ann. Like, really excited."

Luna had lived in New York City before but had purposefully moved back to Whitby. I wasn't totally sure if she wanted to move away again. "What do you make of it? Are you thinking about following him to Charlotte?"

"No. I mean, we could meet up with each other whenever we have time off, of course. But you know how different our schedules are. Sometimes I work weekends. Jeremy never works weekends. And Charlotte is a large city, of course. It's got a totally different rhythm from Whitby."

I nodded, keeping quiet so Luna could talk it out.

"My mom is engaged to be married. I love being near her. And I love my job. Charlotte would mean starting over again from scratch."

I said, "What did Jeremy say when he was telling you about the job? Is he planning on taking it, then?"

"He was so keyed up and excited when he told me. He was already talking about apartments in the South End. It was almost as if he had decided everything without checking in with me first. He assumed I'd be excited too, like of *course* I'd want to leave and follow him to Charlotte. But he didn't ask. He announced."

I said, "It sounds like you're not upset about the offer. It's more that you're upset Jeremy didn't ask how you felt before he got excited about moving." I shook my head. "You know, Grayson and I had to figure out the living situation, too. I didn't really want to leave the cottage, but we knew there wasn't enough space for both of us and our stuff. The addition was our way of compromising."

Luna blinked furiously for a few seconds, looking as if she might cry. I froze up a little, not sure how to handle a crying Luna. She was always so upbeat. Then she said, "Sorry. That's all you needed for your quiet morning was some drama."

I shook my head. "I'm glad you told me. That's really hard. Why don't you sit down with him and tell Jeremy exactly what you told me? That you're not saying no, you're just trying to open up a dialogue with him about it."

"Thanks, Ann. I'll do that." She looked around at the construction. "I hope you know how lucky you are. You've got someone who wanted to build something with you instead of simply expecting you to follow along." She gave me a tight smile. "I better head out. I've got an errand or two to run."

Luna reached out to give me a hug. Her grip was tighter than usual. "Don't tell anyone at work, okay? I'm not ready for Wilson to start planning my farewell party."

"There's nothing to tell. You haven't decided anything."

Luna took a deep breath. "Right. I haven't."

After Luna left, some exercise to unwind seemed like a good idea. I changed clothes, deciding to take a run in the park. Running was definitely not my favorite activity, but it was great for stress relief. I grabbed my earbuds and hopped in the car.

The park was quiet when I arrived, with just a few dog walkers and a mom pushing a jogging stroller. The October air was crisp, and the maples along the trail were starting to turn, displaying patches of orange and red against the blue sky.

I set about stretching at a bench near the trail, working out the tension I hadn't realized I'd been carrying in my shoulders. I'd started on my hamstrings when I noticed a man walking toward me with some purpose. He didn't look threatening, but he definitely seemed like he'd searched me out. I recognized him vaguely. I'd probably seen him around. But then, I'd seen *everyone* around at some point, considering Whitby's size.

He slowed down, maybe realizing his sudden appearance and determined approach might seem alarming. He was in his mid-forties, with the tired eyes and rumpled appearance that came from poor sleep. "Hi there. You're Ann, right? Ann Beckett?"

I nodded. "I'm not sure I've met you."

"Sorry. I'm Tom Cross. I was married to Vivian." He said it as if he was still getting used to the past tense. There was stubble on his face, his jacket was rumpled like it hadn't been hanging up when he put it on, and he had the slightly unfocused look of somebody whose routine has fallen apart. He pointed behind him at the trail. "I was getting some exercise and thought I recognized you from the library." He paused. "I understand you found Vivian."

I nodded again. "That's right. I'm really sorry about Vivian." It looked as if Tom had been hit hard by her death, the investigation into it, or both.

He hesitated as if unsure about what to say or possibly how to say it. "I hope you don't mind me coming up like this. It's just that I've been thinking a lot about Vivian since her death. The cops didn't give me any information at all about what happened to her at Jasper's farmhouse." He sighed. "I get it, but it doesn't help me out at all. I keep envisioning all these horrible things that might have happened to her, and the police won't acknowledge or deny that they did. I know Vivian and I divorced, but I keep worrying she had this really awful violent end to her life. That she suffered." He looked at me with red eyes. "Do you know if she did?"

I immediately said, "No, she definitely didn't. I don't think she was even afraid, surprised, or realized what was going to happen. I can't really disclose any other information than that, since the police probably want to keep all the details from the crime scene quiet. But I can promise you Vivian didn't suffer."

Tom looked suddenly, immensely, relieved. "Oh good. Good. Thank you so much for telling me that. I haven't been able to sleep, worrying about her. I kept feeling like I'd failed her. Like I should have been with her and then this wouldn't have happened. My mind has been spiraling through this whole thing"

"I know it must be awful, losing someone you were once so close to, especially like this. I'm sorry," I said again.

We were quiet for a second. Tom seemed to be lost in memories, although I couldn't tell if they were happy ones or not. We watched a man jog by with a German shepherd running alongside him.

Finally, Tom spoke. "It's been pretty awful, yes. Things weren't always bad between Vivian and me, of course. We were a great match for years and were together for a long time. We met in Charlotte, which anyone will tell you isn't easy to do. It was some sort of networking event." He gave a small smile. "Vivian was ambitious, even back then. She was already chasing the society wedding circuit, and she was terrific at it. She had a great instinct and fantastic taste. And she was so incredibly organized. The only problem was that Vivian couldn't handle anything going wrong."

I said carefully, "I heard about the Morrison wedding. She must have been devastated over that. Vivian sounded like she was a major perfectionist."

Tom gave a wry laugh. "Yes, that's the word for it. She actually made perfectionists look sloppy. But that wedding must have been cursed from the start. Anything that could go wrong, did go wrong. There were multiple disasters." He absentmindedly kicked a stone on the path. "And Vivian's reputation in Charlotte never recovered. So that's why we moved here."

"It wasn't because of a job opportunity you had here?"

Tom said, "No." He gave me a sideways glance, and I saw a flash of something that might have been bitterness. "As a matter of fact, I had to leave a good bank job that I'd been working in Charlotte for twelve years to move to Whitby. I gave it all up because Vivian needed to start over somewhere new. I found work at a smaller bank near here, but it wasn't the same."

"That was a huge sacrifice."

"It was." He shrugged. "I told myself it was the kind of thing you needed to do for someone you love. That we'd figure things out between the two of us, as a team. I may have been over-confident when I figured I could find another banking job or maybe something different here in town." Tom gave a short, humorless laugh. "It turns out Whitby doesn't have a lot of use for mid-level bank managers."

"I'm sure Vivian appreciated that you made the move with her."

He shook his head. "It's really when everything started going wrong between us. I don't think she did appreciate what I was doing. She found it easier to say that I was the one who'd wanted to move to Whitby to start over. Vivian was stubborn about admitting she'd failed in Charlotte. She couldn't admit it to her clients, me, or even to herself. Everything was someone else's fault, whether it was the vendors, the weather, or the clients themselves."

I said, "I'm sure she wasn't used to handling failure at all. It sounds like nothing in her life would have prepared her for that."

Tom looked sad. "Nothing did. And she couldn't figure out how to deal with failure. Then, after a while, I was just another person she blamed for things not being perfect. She thought I wasn't supporting her enough, that I wasn't listening to her, and that I wasn't working hard enough to find work here."

"Which led to the divorce, I'm guessing."

"Right," said Tom. "And the divorce was awful. Vivian got her business and the fresh start. I was snowed under with debt." He shrugged. "I'd found work at a regional bank after we moved here, but I lost that job about six months ago when they merged with a bigger bank. I've been looking for work ever since, but Whitby isn't exactly swimming in opportunities. Despite what Vivian thought, I made finding employment my full-time job."

"What have you been doing with your time?" I asked. I felt myself redden. It came out more directly than I'd intended.

Tom didn't seem offended. "Honestly? Mostly trying not to go crazy." He gestured at the trail around us. "I come here most mornings. I'll walk, or maybe jog sometimes if I'm feeling ambitious. I've read more books in the past six months than the previous ten years. I also taught myself to cook. It turns out I'm terrible at cooking, actually. I tend to get distracted during the process, I guess." He gave a ghost of a smile. "Vivian always handled the meals. She was a great cook when she had the time. That's something people didn't know about her. She was a really creative person in almost every way, even with food."

"What are your next steps now? Are you thinking about moving back to Charlotte? Trying to get your job back over there?"

Tom said, "That's likely the next step, although I don't have a lot of money to make the move. I'd still be paying on my lease here and then having to find another apartment in Charlotte. That's not cheap." He gave a short laugh. "Of course, I can't really do anything while I'm a suspect in a murder investigation."

"Are you feeling like the police are focused on you?"

"Definitely," said Tom, "Although that's probably because I'm her ex-husband. I'd like to think they're not focused on me because I seem guilty." He sighed again. "It's been such a mess. I've been trying to keep healthy and stick with a routine." He waved his hand toward the park. "Exercising helps. When everything falls apart, at least you can control when you get off the couch. Even better, the park is a hundred percent free. My gym membership was one of the first things to go. Like I said, I'm here most mornings."

Tom looked like a guy whose life had imploded. Could he have murdered Vivian, though? He sounded more exhausted than angry.

"Were you able to give the police a good alibi? Shouldn't that keep you from being considered a suspect?"

"Nope. I was home alone. I was sleeping in, since I don't have anywhere to be in the mornings." He spread out his hands.

"I know how it sounds to the cops. I didn't have any witnesses that I was alone at home, which translates into no alibi. But I didn't kill her, Ann. And it's been tough coming to terms with the fact she's gone. We had a lot of really hard words between us over the past year or more, but a part of me still loved the person she was when we'd first met. I'd never have hurt her."

I asked, "Do you have any idea who might have? Had anyone threatened Vivian or had words with her lately?"

Tom gave a bitter laugh. "How long do you have? Unfortunately, Vivian was the kind of person who built herself up by tearing others down."

"Was there anyone specific?"

He thought about it. "That florist in town. Sarah something. Vivian was really hard on her, publicly and repeatedly. I remember she called her arrangements 'amateur hour' during some regional bridal fair. I heard Sarah lost clients because of it."

This didn't surprise me. Vivian had a way of putting down the work of local vendors.

Tom continued. "Vivian went after Sarah especially hard. I'm guessing that's because Sarah's style was the opposite of everything Vivian liked. Sarah's stuff was natural, simple, and local. And I also think Vivian felt threatened by anyone who didn't need fancy to be good."

"Is there anyone else you can think of?"

Tom said, "Well, there was often a trail of unhappy brides wherever Vivian went. That Morrison wedding was her most famous, or infamous, disaster. But there were others. Her brides were often shoehorned into weddings they didn't really want. It was kind of a pattern. Vivian tended to want weddings *her* way, not her clients' way."

Tom quickly glanced at his watch. "I'll let you go. Sorry I kept you from your run. I'm glad you let me know Vivian didn't suffer at the end." He paused. "Look, I know I'm the obvious suspect. I'm an ex-husband with financial problems and no alibi." He spread out his hands. "It's not a great look. But I did really care about Vivian, even after everything. Now I just want to move on. Find a job, start over." He gave me a tired smile. "That's all I've wanted for a long time."

"Thanks for talking with me, Tom."

Tom said, "Thanks for being honest with me." He gave a small wave and headed toward the parking lot.

I watched him go, thinking about what he'd said about the cooking he was trying to learn, his morning walks in the park, and the twelve years at a bank he'd left behind. Tom seemed genuinely concerned about what had happened to Vivian, and he hadn't appeared to be very hung up on his past; it was more like he wanted to move forward. Or was he just very good at covering up his true feelings?

Chapter Eleven

I pulled into my driveway. The October light was a golden slant, warm but with an edge to it. It sort of made everything look like a photograph.

The construction crew looked like they were in full gear. Two trucks were in my small driveway, and I could smell sawdust even before I opened my car door.

I noticed the oak tree in the backyard was starting to turn, and a few leaves drifted down in the breeze. Somewhere, somebody was burning leaves. It was that particular autumn smell that always made me think of my great-aunt raking the yard when I was a kid.

When I walked in, Eddie Greer, the crew lead, was in the front hall, reviewing something on a clipboard. He's a stocky man in his fifties, perpetually dusty, and with a calm confidence I'd come to appreciate over the past few weeks.

"Got a minute?" he asked. "I thought I'd show you some of the progress."

I figured it would be a much more specific tour than the one I took Luna on earlier. I followed him through the plastic sheeting into the addition.

"See here?" Eddie pointed out a spot where the sunroom would connect to the existing cottage. "We got the headers in today. And everything passed inspection thirty minutes ago."

"That's great news."

He said, "We should have the drywall up by the end of the next week, weather permitting." Eddie checked his clipboard. "Your electrician's scheduled for day-after-tomorrow. Assuming there aren't any surprises, we're still on track for the wedding."

"Assuming there aren't any surprises," I said dryly.

Eddie grinned. "In construction, that's what we call optimism." He nodded toward the house. "By the way, your cat's been supervising all day. He's sat in that window for three hours straight. Jake's been sneaking him treats on the sly."

"That would explain why Fitz has been less interested in his supper lately."

He chuckled. "That cat's got the whole grew wrapped around his paw. If he had opposable thumbs, he'd probably be running the job site."

After Eddie got called away by a crew member, I changed from my workout clothes to my favorite worn sweater, comfortable pants, and thick socks because the floors have been chilly sometimes. I put the kettle on and looked out the window. I saw the maple tree across the street had gone fully orange. In another week, it would be bare.

Fitz appeared in the kitchen doorway, stretching elaborately as if he'd had a very difficult morning of window supervision. He padded over and wound between my ankles as a hello before settling onto the kitchen rug to wait for whatever might happen next.

The kettle clicked off, and I made a cup of Earl Gray and carried it into the living room where my book was waiting for me.

I settled into my favorite reading spot; the corner of the sofa where the light is good and there's room for Fitz if he decided to join me. Which he did after a few minutes of checking in again on the construction crew. He hopped up, circled twice, then curled against my thigh, purring before he was even fully settled.

I read for a while, not keeping track of the time. Fitz's purr became a steady, barely audible rumble.

It must have been a couple of hours when my phone buzzed from the side table. I saw Grayson's name and quickly picked up.

"Hey there," I said. Fitz opened one eye at the disturbance before closing it again.

"Hey yourself." There's background noise on his end that sounded like the newsroom hum of phones and conversation. "How's your recharge day going so far?"

"Successfully." I stretched out my free hand to scratch Fitz's ears. "I've accomplished very little that's productive. And it feels great."

"That's the goal." There was a pause on Grayson's end while someone asked him something in the background. I heard him say, "one second" before coming back. "Sorry. Did the crew finish up okay?"

"The drywall and the electrician are next. Eddie says we're still on track."

"Eddie's an optimist," said Grayson.

"That's exactly what I said."

I could hear the smile in Grayson's voice when he said, "I was thinking about Chinese takeout tonight. Does that sound good? I can run by the place near the office that has that soup you like."

"The hot and sour?"

"That's the one," he said.

It somehow made me feel very content that he remembered my favorite foods. "That sounds perfect."

Grayson arrived at the end of the day with bags of Chinese food and some local beer we both liked. We ate on the sofa with the TV on low. It was some home renovation show that neither of us was really watching. Fitz stationed himself on the coffee table, eyeing the containers with cautious interest.

"General Tso's isn't good for cats," advised Grayson gently.

Fitz's expression suggested he disagreed but was willing to let the topic go for now.

"Holly called earlier," I said, reaching for another egg roll. Holly was my college roommate, who I visited in Charleston as much as possible. She was going to be, along with Luna, one of my attendants during the ceremony. "She's driving over the day before the wedding."

"Holly and Luna," said Grayson with a grin. "Now that sounds like an interesting combination."

"Maybe they'll balance each other out," I said, thinking of the preppy, proper Holly and the earth mother Luna.

"Or maybe they won't?"

I said, "Or maybe my wedding morning will involve glitter, a spreadsheet, and possibly a wardrobe change. As an example,

Holly sent me a helpful packing list for our honeymoon. Luna sent me a playlist. I think that tells you everything."

"What was on the playlist?"

"I was afraid to look," I said.

We ate for a few moments. Grayson asked, "How's Holly doing? After everything with Daniel, I mean."

Daniel had been Holly's fiancé. He was a Charleston artist who'd turned out to be better at charming people than actually being a good partner.

"Better, I think. She hasn't mentioned him in months, which is probably a good sign. Oh, before I forget, Holly offered to host us in Charleston sometime after our honeymoon. She says Murphy misses Fitz."

"Does Murphy even remember Fitz?" asked Grayson.

"According to Holly, Murphy remembers everyone he's ever met and loves them all equally and enthusiastically." I smiled. "He's a golden retriever. It's in the job description."

"And Fitz's opinion on this reunion?"

"Being Fitz, I think he'd love it." I paused for a moment. "Holly did say she's excited to see a wedding actually happen. Considering her own engagement fell through, I think she wants to believe in them again."

Grayson reached for my hand. "We can manage that."

The next day was a busy one at the library. I was handling it all well, though, considering I'd had that recharge day. Fitz was being especially fetching, bestowing feline smiles on everyone and getting lots of cuddles in return.

And Fitz was providing excellent stress relief for me, which I sorely needed. My old nemesis, the copier, was at it again. For some reason, a slew of patrons needed it, and the machine was apparently possessed. It jammed, it displayed mysterious error codes, and it printed streaky copies. I was convinced the copier had a personal vendetta against me. It had apparently worked fine yesterday, waiting to act up until my return.

Luna gave me a sad expression as she walked by, although I saw her eyes twinkle with an unholy glee. "So sorry about the copier. I'd help you out, but it seems like you're the only one who has the magic touch with it."

I shook my head. "That's a common misconception among the staff." I carefully opened the panels on the machine and tried to pull out the paper jam. The paper managed to break during the process.

"I'd better go," said Luna, immediately making herself scarce. Which I got; I wouldn't want to help with a broken copier, either.

I finally got the paper out, although I was now covered with printer ink. I made a couple of other adjustments to the machine, which were basically the equivalent of hail-Mary passes. Then, I tried the copier again. It made a ferocious grinding noise. I briefly wondered whether it would be unprofessional to kick it.

Wilson walked up with a concerned look on his face. "How's the copier?"

"What's your copier budget looking like? Because this thing has one foot in the grave."

Wilson made a face. "I'm not sure we really have a copier budget." He looked at me, backing up a couple of paces as if the printer ink covering me might leap over to drench him. "Are you absolutely sure it's not fixed?"

"Well, it made a really scary sound a minute ago."

Wilson reached for a book, opened to a page, then put it face-down on the copier screen. When he hit the start button, it very politely produced a copy. "Great job, Ann," he said, beaming.

I only wished I could have known what I'd done to fix it.

Chapter Twelve

It was a couple of hours later when Jasper Webb found me putting books away in the stacks. I'd been so focused on my task that I blinked at him as if unsure exactly who he was. But then, I was used to seeing my caterer at the farmhouse, not the library. I quickly smiled at him. "Hey there, Jasper. Can I help you find something?"

"Hmm?" he asked, looking distracted. "Oh, right. No, I probably don't need any help." He paused. "Hey, by the way, how are you and Grayson holding up? Weddings are totally chaotic at the best of times. And you've lost your wedding planner."

"We're managing okay, although we've felt bad about Vivian. We're trying to take things as they come, although that can sometimes be tough for me to do."

"That's about all you can do." Jasper leaned against a shelf. "I've been working on a few things for the menu. I thought I might add my grandmother's pecan pie to the dessert table, if you'd like. Grandma always said there's nothing a good pie can't improve."

"That sounds awesome, thanks."

"Good, good." He nodded, but something shifted in his expression. The warmth was still there, but it was edged now with something else. "Actually, I was looking to speak with you. Is this a good time? I'm sorry to bug you at work."

"Sure, now's fine. What's up?"

He took a deep breath. "I hate to bother you about this, Ann, but it's been eating at me. I thought maybe if I could get your take on it, I could put it past me. It seems like the cops think I had something to do with Vivian's death. I mean, I can't even sleep for worrying about it. And maybe my clients do, too. I could really lose customers. Maybe even my business."

Jasper looked both keyed up and exhausted at the same time. "I can't imagine you're a serious suspect. The police are just doing their jobs."

"Have they been questioning you, too?"

I could tell by his hopeful expression that he was hoping I had. But the fact of the matter was that I didn't have a motive to murder Vivian. "No. But I'm sure they're questioning other people, Jasper. Try not to worry about it."

Jasper's face fell, but then he looked hopeful again. "Do you know if there *are* other suspects? I mean, Vivian was murdered at my business, so I guess I'm at the top of the list."

"From what I understand, there are plenty of people who weren't happy with Vivian."

"True," said Jasper. He frowned. "Actually, you reminded me of something. A little over a week ago, I saw Vivian downtown having words with some woman. I was in a rush, picking up supplies, so I just glanced at them. But I remember it was really heated. Vivian was jabbing her finger, the way she did when she was seriously worked up."

"Do you have any idea who it was?"

Jasper shook his head sadly. "I couldn't tell you. Some woman. Maybe she was youngish. I was halfway down the block before I even registered what I was seeing. You know how Vivian was; she argued with everybody. I didn't think much about it."

"Maybe you should let Burton know."

Jasper sighed. "I hate even reminding the cops I exist right now. It just means more questions. But yeah, I'll make a note to call him. Everything seems like such a mess right now. I've had people coming by the farmhouse all week, rubbernecking like it's a tourist attraction or something. One woman's been by a couple of times, gawking. It's very unsettling."

Jasper stopped himself, shaking his head before giving a small, self-conscious laugh. "Listen to me. I sound totally paranoid. Half those cars are probably people parking for the hiking trail." He rubbed the back of his neck. "Mama always said I had an overactive imagination. I saw monsters in every shadow of my room when I was a kid. She'd probably tell me I'm doing the same thing now."

"It doesn't sound paranoid at all to me. There's an actual investigation happening, after all."

Jasper said, "I know. I just keep thinking about Vivian. How someone could . . . do that . . . and then walk away and go on with their day." He looked at me, and I could tell he'd lost some sleep by the redness in his eyes. "I'm not cut out for this murder stuff. I can totally handle a complicated menu, a broken oven, and a hundred guests to feed, but a murder in my farmhouse has really messed me up."

I was about to console him when he waved his hand dismissively. "Anyway, I'm sorry to dump all this on you. You've got enough on your plate with the wedding. I promise I'm still 100% committed to making your day perfect."

"The wedding will be fine. And don't worry about what's going on with the police. Tell me what Burton says if you call him."

Jasper thanked me for listening. It was the kind of thank you that someone gives when they've been carrying something really heavy by themselves and they finally set it down, even briefly.

"You'll call Burton?" I asked.

"I'll call him. You're right. Grandma always said the only way out is through. I might as well handle it directly." He straightened up, his usual warmth returning. "Don't you worry about the food. That's one thing I can guarantee you will be perfect."

He patted my shoulder and headed for the library entrance. At the door, he turned back, giving me a wave.

As planned, Grayson came in with his lunch in a brown paper bag. Mine was in the staff lounge, in the fridge. But my break was starting slightly later than usual.

"Ready for lunch?" asked Grayson, walking up to me.

I gave him a quick smile as I continued surveying the children's section. "In a minute. Maybe. I can unlock the door and let you in the lounge, if you want to get settled."

"Is there anything I can help you with?"

Luna strode up to us, looking frazzled. Her purple-streaked hair was escaping its clip. "Hi Grayson. Sorry, but we have a situation in the children's section."

"What kind of situation?" asked Grayson.

"A frog. A kid actually brought a frog into the library. As if the glitter emergency the other day wasn't enough. And the ridiculous noisemakers."

Grayson frowned. "And the frog is where?"

"That's the situation," said Luna. "We have no idea."

The boy who'd brought in the frog was sitting in a diminutive chair, tears streaking down his face.

"Let me give you a hand," said Grayson, setting his lunch bag down on the top of a row of shelves.

It, of course, was total chaos. The crying frog owner, the children who were loudly and enthusiastically trying to help search, and no sign of the amphibian. We checked behind board-book bins, under tiny chairs, and in the kids' computer area. Nothing.

Finally, I walked over to the puppet theater and peered inside the puppet basket. And there was the frog, looking completely unrepentant and rather sleepy. It was nestled among the hand puppets as if it belonged there.

Grayson then produced a plastic container, formerly used to house craft supplies, and contained the frog safely. The little boy's tears now turned to smiles, and the crisis was averted. For now.

Minutes later, we were eating lunch in the staff lounge. I poured us both a couple of mugs of coffee, figuring we could use it after the frog hunt. Then we settled down to eat our sandwiches.

Grayson said, "I'm hoping that was the only disaster of the day."

"Well, the copier misbehaved, so there was that. Aside from those two things, it's been fine. Oh, Jasper came to see me this morning."

"Really? What, about the food for the wedding?" asked Grayson.

"No, actually, he was worried about whether the police were treating him as a major suspect or not. He seemed to be hoping I'd been questioned by the cops as much as he apparently has."

Grayson gave me a wry look. "I'm sure you weren't able to relieve his mind on that score."

"Exactly. I just don't have a motive. I was there with Jasper when we found Vivian, but that's the extent of my involvement. Vivian's death didn't help me out in any way."

Grayson said, "If anything, it made your life more complicated. Do you think Jasper's being sensitive? Or is there something there? Do the police really think he's the murderer?"

"Who knows? But Jasper did mention he'd witnessed an argument between Vivian and some other woman a week or so ago. He couldn't identify the woman, though, so it's not a lot of help."

"Did he say anything else useful?" Grayson took a bite of his sandwich.

"Only that someone's been hanging around the farmhouse, rubbernecking. He seemed like he was rattled by the whole thing." I paused, remembering. "Oh, and I forgot to tell you last night that I ran into Tom Cross yesterday morning at the park. That's Vivian's ex-husband."

Grayson grinned at me. "And here I was so impressed by your quiet day off yesterday."

"It *was* a quiet day off! But after I did a suspect interview while exercising at the park." I smiled back at him.

"How did it go?"

I said, "He approached me, actually. He was looking for information about how Vivian died. He told me the police weren't giving him anything."

"Which isn't surprising. What kind of information was he looking for? The murder weapon?"

I said, "Nothing like that. It was more that he wanted to make sure Vivian hadn't been afraid or suffered at the end. I was able to relieve his mind on that. There's no way she ever knew what hit her." I took a sip of my coffee. "Tom sounded like he was really struggling. He lost his job at the bank after the merger. Now he's wanting to move back to Charlotte but isn't sure he can afford the move. And, of course, he's still a suspect, since he didn't have an alibi for the police. But he said he didn't do it."

Grayson asked, "Do you believe him?"

"I believe he's exhausted and bitter. But whether that means he's guilty or just worn down, I couldn't tell you. He said there should be plenty of suspects for Vivian's murder. That she left a trail of unhappy brides wherever she went."

Grayson said, "Okay. So we've got Sarah Chen, our florist; Jessica Morton, the bride with the wedding disaster; Tom Cross, Vivian's ex; the wedding planner Patricia Holbrook; and Jasper, our caterer, all on the list." Grayson shook his head. "That's a lot of people who weren't sorry to see Vivian gone."

"And maybe the woman Jasper saw downtown. The one arguing with Vivian. It could be another of Vivian's former brides." I frowned. "I told him to call Burton about it."

"Do you think he will?"

"I hope so," I said. "Jasper seemed reluctant to remind the police he exists."

There was a scratching sound at the lounge door. Grayson raised his eyebrows. "One of the kids from the children's section wanting in?"

"No, I have the feeling I know who that is." I opened the door and Fitz bounded in, looking very pleased with himself for having gotten into the inner sanctum. He rubbed his entire side against me, then looked hopefully at my sandwich.

"It's a peanut butter and jelly," I said. "You're a carnivore."

Fitz's expression seemed to assure me he could easily adapt to being an omnivore. I found some cat treats in the cabinet under the sink, which appeared to suffice.

Because I'd opened up the library, I was off by mid-afternoon. I scooped up Fitz, put him in his carrier, and headed home for tea and reading. It was good to have a break after the various bits of chaos at work.

Around four o'clock, my phone rang. I frowned as I saw it was Mona. I remembered she and Wilson had left the library before I did, planning on going bird-watching together. Mona had been pushing Wilson to find activities they could both do together.

"Mona?" I asked. "Is everything okay?"

Her voice was exceedingly calm on the other end. But Mona wasn't usually that steady. "It's . . . well, Wilson and I are fine."

"What's wrong?"

Mona said, "It's Jasper Webb. He's dead, Ann. Someone killed him."

Chapter Thirteen

The words didn't make sense to me at first. I'd just been talking to Jasper at the library, only hours ago. In the stacks.

"Burton's here now," said the unfamiliar, calm Mona. "But I thought you'd like to know. And maybe Burton wants to talk to you. I saw you with Jasper earlier today at the library. Maybe Jasper had some information you could share? Anyway, we're at the trailhead near the farmhouse. You know, the Ridgeline Trail."

"I'm on my way." I was already grabbing my keys.

I called Grayson in the car, but ended up getting his voicemail, which I left a message on. When I arrived at the farmhouse, there were already a couple of emergency vehicles there. I saw Wilson's car parked on the side of Ridgeline Road and pulled in behind him. Burton's cruiser blocked the gravel lot, presumably to keep others from parking there.

Wilson was pale and shaken. Mona had tucked her arm through his. I saw Burton talking with another officer, who was stretching crime scene tape at the trailhead. On the other side of the tape, I could see a form on the ground near the first bend of the trail. It looked like Jasper. His hand weights were nearby.

I could tell Wilson was trying to rally. "Ann. Thank you for coming." He sounded as if he were hosting a library event.

"Are you two okay?" I asked. "What happened?"

Wilson looked over at Mona. She answered for him. "We were looking for woodpeckers. We've been trying to track what we've spotted, and we haven't had any luck with woodpeckers."

Wilson cleared his throat. "We've heard them, but we haven't seen them. Or taken pictures of them."

"We were heading for the trail when we saw Jasper lying there," said Mona, looking somber. She gave Wilson a squeeze.

Wilson said slowly, "I thought he'd just fallen down at first. That maybe he stepped into one of those groundhog holes and twisted his ankle. Or broke it or something."

Mona nodded. "Or that maybe he'd had some kind of medical emergency, although he seemed too young to have that." She swallowed. "We think he was hit on the head by one of his hand weights."

"Did you see anyone else?" I asked. "On the trail or in the parking lot? Jasper said earlier that there had been lots of people parking outside the farmhouse to stare at the murder site."

"That's obnoxious," said Mona, sounding aggravated on Jasper's behalf. "But no, there was no one else here. At least, not that I noticed. You didn't see anyone, did you, Wilson?"

He shook his head, still looking rather pale. "It was pretty quiet. That's why we chose this time. If there were a lot of people on the trail, it might have scared the birds away." He sighed. "But if we'd come earlier, maybe Jasper wouldn't be dead."

Mona said, "Don't think that way. It might not have changed anything. Or the killer might have murdered *us*, too."

Burton finished speaking with the cop, then headed our way, looking tired. Two murders in the space of a week. "Hi Ann. Mind if I ask you a few questions for a minute? Mona was saying you talked with Jasper earlier today."

"Do you need us to give you some space?" asked Wilson.

"No, it's fine," I said. "It wasn't a private conversation. Well, I suppose it *was*, but it's nothing that can't be shared. Yes, Jasper came to the library while I was shelving books. He was worried he was being considered a major suspect by the police. And that he might lose clients."

Burton frowned. "I don't think we've spent more time questioning Jasper than we had anybody else who might have had information."

"He was probably just sensitive. At any rate, he was worried. Then he started telling me about seeing Vivian arguing with a woman downtown."

Burton pulled out a small notebook. "When was that?"

"It sounded like it was a week before Vivian died. He wasn't able to give any details about the woman, though. Jasper said it struck him as kind of 'business as usual' for Vivian. He acted like an argument with Vivian was something so unremarkable that he didn't even pay too much attention to it. He was busy getting supplies for his business at the time, so he was in a hurry."

Burton jotted some notes down. "Okay. Anything else?"

"He did mention having a lot of gawkers at the farmhouse. He put it down to rubbernecking, although he said something about a woman being there twice." I gave a small shiver. Everything Jasper had said, which had sounded innocuous enough then, now seemed ominous to me.

Burton looked at me. "Did Jasper say he was going to talk to anyone else about this?"

"I told him to give you a call."

Burton said, "He didn't."

I felt a sinking sensation in my stomach. If Jasper had called Burton, would he still be alive? Had he inadvertently tipped off his killer instead of talking to the police?

Mona reached over to pull me into a one-armed hug. "None of this is your fault, is it, Burton?" She gave Burton a ferocious look, like a mama bear defending her cub.

"Of course not," said Burton. "It was up to Jasper to share any information he had. The only person responsible for his death is the murderer."

A couple of sedans pulled onto the street. "The state police are here," said Burton. "I'll reach back out to all of you if I need more information."

It was definitely a dismissal. But then I saw the state police weren't the only vehicles on their way over. Grayson was driving up too.

He hopped out and strode over to us, a notebook in his hand. "Everybody okay?"

Wilson said gruffly, "Yes. A lot better than poor Jasper is."

Grayson shook his head. "What a mess. What were you and Mona doing here? And don't worry, this is off-the-record."

Wilson cleared his throat. "Birdwatching, actually It's a fairly new activity for us."

"But fun," said Mona. "We get outside. And it's kind of like this competitive game. We take pictures of the different birds we see and share them online with other birders." She gestured to the trail. "We didn't get far before we ran into Jasper."

Wilson apparently didn't want to do more rehashing. "Let's go back to my house, Mona. The police are finished with us. I think I could do with a cup of coffee."

"I think we could do with something stronger than that," said Mona.

Grayson and I watched as they left. Grayson said, "I'm so sorry, Ann. I really liked Jasper."

"So did I." I took a deep breath. "And, like I told you at lunch, I just talked to him this morning. He was so worried about everything. But he was also reassuring me he was going to do this awesome job on our catering." My voice caught a little, and I waited for a second before I filled him in on my conversation with Jasper.

"Do you think he ended up confronting his killer?" asked Grayson.

I thought about this. "It didn't seem like he had any idea of the identity of the woman who'd been arguing with Vivian. And maybe it was unrelated. Like Jasper said, Vivian was always arguing with somebody. Maybe Jasper knew something else, maybe even something he didn't *realize* he knew. Maybe the killer couldn't take the chance Jasper would remember."

Burton stepped away from his conversation with the state police, and Grayson said, "I'd better grab the chance to talk to the chief. Can I catch up with you later?"

I nodded, and he gave me a quick hug before hurrying away.

The rest of the day was a blur. I went home to snuggle with Fitz for a while. I even ate a bowl of soup, I guess for the pure comfort of it. Grayson came by briefly around eight p.m. to check in on me before rushing off again to make sure the story was ready for the paper the next morning. And I had a restless and unsatisfying night's sleep.

It was almost a relief to go to work the next day. There was something about the normality that really appealed. And Fitz, as always, was delighted to be there. Maybe he'd been influenced by the frog incident (which I remember him watching with interest), but he'd discovered the puppet basket was a marvelous place for napping.

I was at the circulation desk, filling in for a library tech who'd called in sick, when Sarah Chen walked in. She was carrying a small flower arrangement in fall colors of rust, gold, and a deep burgundy. Her expression seemed troubled, or maybe distracted. I gave her a small wave, and she walked over to me, setting the arrangement on the counter between us. "Hey there," she said. "Is Luna around? These are for her."

The flowers were beautiful, the kind of thing Sarah did so well. They were wildflowers that looked like they'd been gathered from a meadow, even though I knew she'd arranged every stem deliberately.

I realized that, with everything going on, I hadn't followed up with Luna on how her conversation with Jeremy had gone. Was he still intent on moving to Charlotte? Did he still expect her to join him? If he was the one sending the flowers, it looked like maybe their talk hadn't gone as well as it might have.

"I think Luna's on break right now, but I can give them to her."

Sarah nodded, but I could tell she wasn't really listening. It looked as if she had something on her mind. She glanced around to see if anyone was within earshot, but it had been an unexpectedly quiet morning so far at the library. There were a few regulars at the computers and an elderly man browsing the large-print section. "Do you have a minute, Ann?"

Chapter Fourteen

"Sure. What's up?" I continued checking in books while we talked.

Sarah said quietly, "I heard about Jasper. And I saw the story in the paper this morning. I just can't believe it. I mean, Jasper of all people."

"I know."

She shook her head slowly. "He brought me biscuits once. It seemed like a really simple thing, but it was so sweet. I'd had a terrible week that week. I'd lost two arrangements because of a power outage and had a bride scream at me over the phone like I'd done it on purpose. Jasper called up to check on me because he was catering for the same bride and had heard her venting about me." Sarah's voice caught. "He showed up at the shop with a basket of biscuits and a jar of his grandmother's strawberry jam. He said he thought I might be able to use some comfort food. He didn't even stay. He dropped them off, gave me a hug, and left."

"That sounds like Jasper."

She continued, "He was the nicest guy in town. I mean, ask anyone and they'd say the same. Ask *anyone*. I was working on an event with him one time. It was one of those really stressful ones with a bridezilla. I was totally stressed out. I remember Jasper was so kind to me. Even though he was handling the catering, he took the time to tell me some funny stories about past weddings. I was so much more relaxed. Which was good, since I'd felt like I was going to have a panic attack at the time."

I could see her face and neck were getting blotchy with anger. Sarah said, "First Vivian. And fine, Vivian made enemies. I could totally see someone wanting to harm her. But Jasper? Who hurts Jasper?"

It looked like Sarah needed an ear more than anything else. I nodded. "I know. Jasper was the best. Like you said, it's hard to wrap my head around."

A couple of patrons walked up like they might ask me to check out their books for them before deciding to try self-checkout.

Sarah continued, "And now the police are probably going to make their rounds again. I'm so sick of all this, Ann. The cops need to buckle down and figure out who's behind this. Otherwise, the killer could strike again, you know? Who knows who could be next?"

I said, "You're probably right about the police asking more questions."

Sarah gave a scoffing laugh. "And, once again, I didn't have the foresight to have an alibi. I was out making deliveries all day in the van. So it's not like I wasn't out and about."

It at least sounded like her business was picking up. "Were you near the farmhouse at all?"

"Actually, I got fairly close to it. I was driving past the old Mercer place, near the trail out there." She frowned, her fingers finding a stray leaf on the counter and turning it over absently. "As a matter of fact, I saw somebody else out there. I didn't think anything about it at the time. But Tom Cross was out that way. His truck was pulled off on the shoulder, and he was just sitting there."

"When was this?"

Sarah thought about it. "Let's see. It would have been early morning, I guess. It was after I grabbed breakfast on the road. I'm not sure of the exact time because I was already running behind on deliveries, even though it was early, and I was stressed. I almost stopped because I thought maybe Tom had broken down. But he wasn't looking under his hood or anything like that. He was sitting there, sort of staring off into space. So I kept going."

"You're sure it was him?"

"Definitely. I looked right at him, and he didn't even notice. I mean, I could be wrong about the time, but I know what I saw."

"You'll let Burton know about that?" My voice was more insistent this time than it had been during my conversation with Jasper the day before. I didn't want Sarah to be the next victim.

"I'll call him as soon as I leave here," she said. She made a face. "I hope I'm not going to make the police suspicious about Tom. Maybe he was only trying to chill out over there."

"Did Tom spot you looking at him?"

Sarah said, "No, I don't think so. He looked like he was really exhausted or something. Like I said, he was looking off into space. At nothing." She shrugged. "Maybe he was resting after being on the trail? Catching his breath? Who knows."

I changed course a little. "Hey, I'm sorry about Jasper. It sounds like you knew him well."

Sarah paused. "Well, we were colleagues, in a way. We'd see each other at events and at markets. In this town, everybody knows everyone. And I had a lot of respect for Jasper. He had such a big, friendly personality."

"Did you ever see him have any kind of disagreement with anyone?"

Sarah's pause was a little longer this time. She sighed. "Well, I did. It was minor, though. And work-related."

"What was it about?"

Sarah said, "I had this idea, maybe six months ago. I thought a local wedding package would be a great idea to drum up business. It would have my flowers, Jasper's catering, and maybe Patricia's planning, if she came around. Then we could bundle it together as an alternative to Vivian's expensive out-of-town imported vendors."

"That's actually not a bad idea."

"Right?" asked Sarah. "I thought it made sense. Maybe we could have looped Jasper's farmhouse in, too, as a venue. It would be local vendors supporting each other and keeping business in town instead of watching it go outside Whitby."

"But Jasper didn't go for it?"

Sarah shook her head. "I pitched it to him first. I thought he'd be an easy yes. I mean, he totally heard me out. He was very polite, like he usually was. And then he said no. He wanted to stay independent, without getting locked into any arrangements. He said he wanted to keep his business model simple."

Sarah's voice was matter-of-fact, but I could hear an edge to it. She continued. "I kind of took it personally, which wasn't at all what he meant by it. It's just that I thought he'd see the value in our businesses sticking together. But I got over it. We were fine after that, totally cordial."

"Still, it must have stung," I said.

She shrugged. "It did. But it wasn't a huge deal. I tried to look at it as a small setback. And now I feel like an idict about ever being upset with him over something that wasn't that important to begin with."

"Did anyone else know about this disagreement you had with Jasper?"

Sarah gave a short laugh. "In this town? Probably everybody. I wasn't quiet about my disappointment at the time. Patricia definitely knew, since she was part of the pitch I made. I'm sure Burton will hear about it eventually, if he hasn't already. But, look. I would never have hurt Jasper. Ever. I was behaving a little cool to Jasper after that, which I'm kicking myself over now. I can't take my attitude back." She took a deep breath. "Anyway, I don't think I knew Jasper quite as well as I should have. I should have been a better friend to him. But also, I think he was the kind of person who kept troubles to himself."

"Do you think Jasper had a lot on his mind lately?" I asked. I remembered how he'd seemed yesterday in the library. He was worried about the police being suspicious of him, and he seemed really on edge overall.

"I'm sure he had stuff on his mind, yes. I saw him out a couple of days ago, and he seemed really distracted. Sort of off. At first, I thought it might be because I'd been such a pill to him about the business bundle I'd pitched him. But it didn't seem like that was it." She shook her head. "I should have pushed him to talk. Maybe whatever it was that was on his mind was what ended up getting him killed."

I said, "You mentioned Patricia the last time we talked. That Vivian had called her work 'quaint.' Have you spoken to her recently?"

Sarah made a face. "I didn't mean to make it sound like Patricia did anything to Vivian. And I sure can't see her killing Jasper. I know she was crazy about him. She was always recommending his catering to her clients. But no, she's not returning my calls."

"So you don't think Patricia should be considered a suspect?"

"I know I said she had motive. And she did. After all, Vivian stole her clients and damaged her reputation by putting down her planning services. But it's tough to imagine, isn't it? Unless she got really fired up at Vivian and acted in the heat of the moment. As for Jasper, it seems like whoever did that was scared. They must have had something to hide and were trying to cover it up."

I said, "Thinking about Vivian's clients, Grayson and I talked to Jessica Morton. She was the bride whose wedding fell apart. She actually reached out to Grayson at the paper and wanted to tell her story."

"Oh, that poor girl. I remember that wedding. I wasn't the florist, thankfully, because Vivian brought in someone from Charlotte. I heard about it, though, like everybody else."

I asked, "Do you remember the details of what happened?"

"Mostly. It was stuff like the flowers being the wrong color or variety, the cake being late or never arriving, and the photographer walking out. Vivian, naturally, blamed everyone but herself." Sarah shook her head. "The poor bride, though. I heard her marriage didn't last, either. Can you imagine? Her wedding day was ruined, then her marriage fell apart, too."

I shook my head. This was the first I heard about Jessica's marriage ending. I wondered if that was something Jessica blamed Vivian for. That their lives together had gotten off on the wrong foot. Sometimes it was tough to stop blaming people once you got started.

I tuned back into what Sarah was saying, which seemed to be something about Vivian's ex-husband.

"Tom Cross," I said.

"Right. He's the obvious suspect, am I right? I mean, sure Vivian annoyed a lot of the vendors that she worked with. And maybe she upset a few brides along the way. But Tom was married to Vivian. You never really know what goes on in someone's private life."

I asked, "Did you ever hear Vivian talk about her marriage?"

"Oh, yeah. She was always complaining about him. Vivian acted like he was this really low-energy, unmotivated guy. But it sounded to me more of a case of opposites attracting, to me. Vivian was a driven, Type-A person. Can you imagine if she'd married someone just like her?" She gave a short laugh. Then she looked at her watch, frowning. "Okay, I'd better run. I've got some arrangements to deliver for the funeral service. Are you going?"

"Vivian's service? I didn't know anything about it."

Sarah said, "Her brother, who lives on the west coast, has come into town. It's a visitation at the funeral home tomorrow morning at ten. He's going to have a private memorial service and burial with just family a couple of days from now. But the public is welcome to the funeral home."

"I'll definitely be there."

Chapter Fifteen

As Sarah headed out of the library, I saw Luna was visible in the children's section again. I picked up the arrangement and headed over. "Special delivery," I said with a smile.

Luna glanced up from the shelving, and her whole face softened. "From Jeremy?"

"I'm guessing," I said.

Luna's whole face softened. She reached for the tiny envelope first, sliding out the card inside. Her smile grew as she read it.

"Good news?" I asked.

"It says, 'I'm sorry I didn't listen. Can we talk?'" Luna tucked the card back in the envelope. She studied the arrangement, which was in a simple mason jar. There were black-eyed Susans, purple coneflowers, and a spray of something I couldn't identify. They were wild, asymmetrical, and beautiful.

She took the jar and walked a few feet to her desk. She adjusted it so it caught the light in a sunbeam. She was still looking at the flowers as she said, "Jeremy and I did talk about the move. Or, we argued, I guess." She turned to look at me. "Honestly, Ann, I felt like I was taking a teddy bear away from a little kid. He's *so* excited about moving to Charlotte. And I'm just . . . not."

"Jeremy took it badly, then?"

"You could say that," Luna said, blowing out a gusty sigh. "Ugh. I wasn't going to blurt out my feelings like that. I'd practiced, Ann, really I had. I was going to be gently supportive, then tell him I was very disappointed he hadn't asked me what I wanted. That he expected me to pack up and follow him."

"But it didn't come out that way."

"Nope," said Luna. "Although, to be fair, I'd listened to a ten-minute monologue of him talking about apartments in Charlotte, the job itself, and places we could hang out in the city. He wasn't consulting with me on anything. On the upside, he was so very happy. Sooo enthusiastic. Then I rained right on his parade."

"You had to say something," I pointed out.

"You're totally right. And believe me, I did. I told him I couldn't believe he hadn't asked me what I wanted. That we were *not* the same person, and he couldn't pretend to know my feelings unless he asked about them, which he certainly hadn't. And then I pointed out I was happy here in Whitby. I'd moved from New York City, for heaven's sake. I'd done a big city previously, and I'd decided a small town, with the quirky people, near my mom was what I wanted."

"What did he say to that?"

Luna had to smile at that. "Well, Jeremy didn't say anything at first. He kind of turned an alarming red color. His mouth was opening and closing, but no words were coming out. It was pretty comical. But I was careful not to laugh."

"Did he finally get his voice back?"

"Sadly," said Luna. "He was very defensive. I guess I can't blame him. From his point of view, my tirade came out of nowhere. But he fired back some stuff. He said he was hurt that I wasn't happy for him. I told him I *was* happy for him. The problem was that he expected me to drop everything. Anyway, he ended up storming out."

"Was your mom there?" I asked. Luna still lived at her mom's house. But then, Mona was going to be moving in with Wilson after the wedding.

"No, thankfully. She was out with Wilson. Mom loves Jeremy. She'd be so disappointed if we broke up."

I looked down at the flowers. "No chance of that. It looks like Jeremy wants to make up."

Luna smiled. "It does look that way."

"Are you going to call him?"

Which was when Luna's phone buzzed. She smiled again as Jeremy's name popped up on her screen.

I smiled, leaving her to take her call, and headed over to the community room to set up for the library's film club. It was one of my favorite groups. All the regulars had been there for years. I arranged the chairs so they faced the TV and got the popcorn machine started. Luna had taken it upon herself to extend the October decorations to the community room after she'd decorated the children's section, so there was a mix of fall and Halloween decorations.

Fitz padded in behind me. Film club was one of his favorite library activities, too. Everyone hoped he'd pick their lap to nap in, and he tried to spread out his attention with different laps each month.

Luna came bustling in a few minutes later, a smile on her face.

"Is that smile because of Jeremy, or because of film club?" I asked, grinning.

She gave me a smug look. "Both." She absentmindedly picked glitter from her hair. Knowing Luna, I'd thought it was there intentionally, but it was apparently the result of a craft mishap in the children's area. She looked at the glitter in her hand. "I do love kids, but I'm glad to spend some time with grown-ups right now. I wouldn't mind hearing normal problems in normal conversation. Problems that don't involve anyone asking why the sky is blue fourteen times in a row."

"I could probably come up with a problem," I said.

"Please. I need to remember that conversations have actual conclusions sometimes."

I loaded Luna's film for playing and said in a carefully casual voice. "So how did your conversation with Jeremy go? I'm guessing you called him?"

"Oh, that. Yeah, he was apologetic."

I smiled. "I figured, considering the flowers. What else did he say?"

A small smile tugged at her lips. "Jeremy's going to ask the guy who hired him if he'll consider remote work, instead. So fingers crossed. I mean, maybe it won't work out, but it would be awesome if it did." She paused.

There seemed to be something else there, so I waited a few beats.

Luna sighed. "In the excitement of the moment and the fact that he is going to see if he can work remotely, I might have told him I loved him." She paused. "Unfortunately."

"Unfortunately?"

Luna said, "I wasn't planning on having *feelings*. Especially any strong ones. I didn't want to rearrange my life around another person, you know. It's very inconvenient." She plopped into one of the folding chairs. "As you'll remember, I moved back from New York to get away from complicated. Whitby was supposed to be easy with a library job, weird patrons, Mom, and maybe a bunch of cats in my future. Peaceful."

"And then Jeremy came along."

Luna nodded. "Yes. Jeremy came along with his optimism and his flowers and his total willingness to restructure his career because I said I didn't want to move."

"That sounds good, though. Right?"

Luna scowled at me as if I hadn't been paying close attention. "It's terrifying. What if I mess it up? I always mess relationships up. What if Jeremy resents me later for holding him back from moving to Charlotte?" She stopped, taking a deep breath. "Sorry, I tend to spiral."

"Spiraling is allowed," I said.

"Anyway, enough of my drama. You're getting married, like, practically immediately. How are you not completely losing it?"

"Who says I'm not?" I said with a smile.

"You look annoyingly calm. Is that a librarian thing? Serene in the face of chaos? I guess it must not be, considering I'm a librarian, too."

I said, "It's probably more of a 'too tired to panic' thing."

"Valid." Luna leaned forward in her folding chair. "Okay, what do you need? And before you say 'nothing,' I'm going to help whether you like it or not. I've been pretty useless during this whole murder-wedding disaster business, and I have guilt."

"You haven't been useless."

"I've been distracted," said Luna. "Distracted by all my own drama. While you've been out finding bodies, interviewing suspects, and somehow still planning a wedding." She snapped her fingers. "I've got it. I'm your attendant, so I should attend."

"I think you've already RSVP'd."

"Yes, but I mean really be sort of an old-fashioned attendant, the kind who actually does stuff. Sort of like a lady-in-waiting," said Luna.

I managed not to smile at the image of Luna with her multi-colored glitter hair playing the role of a lady-in-waiting.

Luna continued. "So I'll help you get ready the morning of the wedding. This is non-negotiable. Someone needs to make sure you actually eat breakfast and don't pace around being nervous."

"Actually, that would be a big help," I admitted. "You could give me a hand behind the scenes. Just sort of coordinating everything, too. Making sure everything else is going well."

Luna grinned. "Consider it done. I'm excellent at coordinating. I coordinate toddlers, Ann. Weddings are nothing. What else?"

"That's probably it. We're keeping it simple."

Luna said, "I totally approve of keeping things simple. That's very on-brand for you two. Grayson's probably relieved he doesn't have to wear a fancy suit."

"He's wearing a nice suit, actually. But it will still be laid-back."

Luna said warmly, "Hey, I'm really happy for you. And Grayson, too. The two of you together are just so good."

"Thanks, Luna."

"And I'm sure at this rate the murders will be solved before the wedding. That could be really awkward, otherwise. 'Dearly beloved, we are gathered here . . . oops, the killer's in row three."

I chuckled. "I don't think we've invited any of the suspects."

The film club started filing in, and Luna immediately stepped back into full Luna mode. "You're all going to love this movie," she proclaimed.

Timothy was walking in with Owen. "What is it?" he asked with a grin.

"You'll have to wait for the announcement like everyone else," said Luna. "I'm anticipating the reveal. After all, this is the first time I've picked a film."

Zelda, who was a relative newcomer to the group, gave a snort as if she'd reserve judgment on the title after she heard it.

Everyone grabbed a bag of popcorn and settled into their seats, chatting together for a few minutes before I called the club to order and introduced Luna to anyone who didn't already know her.

Luna stood up in front of the group. "Okay, so I picked this month's movie. Don't judge me."

"I'd never judge a film pick. That's sacred," said Timothy.

"It's not exactly obscure cinema. Or artsy."

Zelda breathed a sigh of relief.

Luna said, "And maybe it didn't win awards. Well, maybe it did, who knows." She stopped, waving a hand. "You know what? Just watch it."

She propped up the movie poster she'd printed out onto an easel.

George, a regular who owned the typewriter repair shop on the square said, "The Addams Family! Classic."

Luna gave him a thumbs-up. "It's October, right? And I needed a reminder that functional relationships can look completely insane from the outside and still work. Also, Morticia's wardrobe is amazing. Obviously."

Zelda was frowning, trying to place the movie. "Is this the one with the hand?"

"Thing!" said Owen. "Yeah, he's great."

"Hmph. We'll see," said Zelda.

I dimmed the lights and settled into my usual spot near the back. Fitz blinked at me from George's lap before falling asleep. Luna eagerly watched everyone's reactions to the film as it unfolded. She looked pleased as we all laughed at Wednesday's deadpan lines. Mona beamed at Wilson during Morticia and Gomez's romantic moments. Zelda snorted at the chaos in the movie but seemed clearly entertained.

At the end, everybody clapped. Luna looked relieved at the reception.

"Solid pick, Luna," said Timothy. "The thing I really love about this movie is that the Addams family isn't the problem. Everyone *else* is the problem. The family is actually really healthy."

"Right?" said Luna. "They're weird, but they're not dysfunctional. They work."

George, who was still absently petting Fitz, said, "Morticia and Gomez have a better marriage than the stuff I've seen on romcoms."

Mona added, "They really do. All that passion after all those years."

Wilson looked somewhat pink. "They do seem quite devoted."

Luna said, "What did you make of it, Zelda?"

"That Wednesday kid doesn't put up with any nonsense. She knows exactly who she is. That's not nothing."

Owen gave Zelda a small thumbs-up for participating. Then he said, "And they accept everybody, you know? Like Cousin Itt just shows up and they're like, 'Oh good, Itt's here.' No questions asked."

I said, "They've kind of built their own normal, haven't they? The rest of the world thinks they're strange, but inside that house, everything makes sense."

"Okay," said Luna. "Well, thanks for coming, everybody! And next month someone else is picking. I've done my part for cinema. And the library."

"I've got some ideas," said Timothy.

"Something with action next time," said Zelda. "All that romance made me antsy."

Owen said, "You *liked* it, Miss Zelda."

"I tolerated it. There's a difference. It was certainly better than that movie where they were walking around Rome the whole time."

"So you'll come next month?" asked Owen.

"Depends on what's showing. But probably," groused Zelda.

Everyone threw away their popcorn bags and helped me fold their chairs and put them away as they chatted and caught up with each other. Fitz had allowed George to move and had curled back up on the warm spot where he'd been sitting, his eyes half-closed in contentment, one ear swiveling to track the conversation.

Mona gave Luna a hug. "That was a lovely pick. Very romantic."

Luna said, "Don't tell anyone, Mom. I have a reputation, you know."

"Your secret's safe with me."

Mona looked over at Wilson. "You enjoyed it too, didn't you?"

"I did. I needed something lighthearted." He paused. "Actually, I look forward to film club. It exposes me to a lot of movies I'd never have picked for myself."

People filtered out and I finished cleaning up the room.

Chapter Sixteen

The rest of the afternoon passed quietly. After my shift at the library wrapped up, Grayson had me over to his place for a spaghetti supper. His kitchen smelled of garlic and tomatoes, and he'd already poured two glasses of wine.

"I don't know how you even had the time to make this," I said. "You've got to be slammed at the paper right now."

He grinned at me. "I made it in the pressure cooker, so it was sort of cheating, really. The uncooked noodles and everything else went in there together. It was done in like thirty minutes. Hope that hasn't spoiled your mental picture of me sweating over a hot stove."

"No, it makes me feel better, actually."

We sat together in comfortable quiet, eating our pasta while jazz music played softly in the background.

"Did you have a good day?" he asked.

"I did. Oh, before I forget, the funeral home visitation for Vivian is tomorrow morning. But then, you might have already known about that, if it was printed in the paper."

Grayson shook his head. "There's nothing in the paper about it. The family must have only listed the information on the funeral home site."

"Are you going?"

Grayson shook his head. "Unfortunately, I have a physical scheduled for tomorrow morning. And the appointment is right in the middle of the morning at 9:30. Guessing that won't work out."

"The visitation is at 10:00."

"Gotcha. I'll just let you represent me at it," said Grayson. "I do feel bad about Vivian. She could be a pain to deal with, but she didn't deserve what happened to her. Do you know who organized the visitation? Was it Vivian's ex?"

"Sarah told me it was her brother. He flew in from the west coast, apparently."

Grayson twirled spaghetti around his fork. "I didn't know she had a brother. But then, I didn't know much about Vivian outside of wedding planning mode."

"I get the feeling not many people did."

We ate in silence for a few moments. The jazz shifted to something with a lazy trumpet line.

"By the way, I talked to Jeremy today," said Grayson. "He reached out at lunch to see if I could grab a bite with him."

I hadn't even had the chance to tell Grayson Luna's thoughts on Jeremy's job offer and move. I was interested to see what Jeremy had said. "Were you able to join up?"

"Yeah, I took an hour off. He was very preoccupied." Grayson reached for the Parmesan. "Jeremy said he'd gotten a great job offer in uptown Charlotte, working for one of the big banks. He said it was a great opportunity for him with better pay and more room to grow." Grayson shrugged. "But he didn't sound all that excited. Apparently, he and Luna had an argument about it."

I nodded. "Luna mentioned that."

"He was saying that he wasn't sure where he really wanted to be. He asked how I knew Whitby was the right place for me. It's a small town with a smaller newspaper, of course. He was curious whether I'd ever thought of going somewhere bigger."

"What did you tell him?" I asked.

"That I'd thought about it, but then I'd realized I wasn't choosing between a big career and a smaller one. I was choosing a lifestyle." He took a sip of his water. "It wasn't really about the job. It was about the whole situation. That maybe he needed to consider the big picture, too."

"Meaning Luna?"

"Meaning everything. Luna, Whitby, putting down roots." Grayson shrugged. "Just figuring out what was most important to him."

"Well, I hope everything works out. I don't know how serious the two of them are, but I think it would be tough to have a long-distance relationship. Oh, I did hear from Luna today that Jeremy is going to ask if he can work the job remotely."

Grayson said, "Really? That would be the perfect solution, if it works out."

"It sounded like Jeremy wasn't sure if that was on the table or not. Or maybe the bank would want him in Charlotte a couple of days out of the week. I'd imagine that would be a deal-breaker, considering the distance."

Grayson said, "I hope it works out. Luna and Jeremy make a great couple. I'll see if I can give him a call later and hear him out about all this."

I reached over and squeezed his hand. "You're a good friend."

"I try." He squeezed back. "Now eat your pasta before it gets cold. I didn't spend thirty whole minutes on this food for nothing."

The next morning, I headed to Vivian's visitation. Even though Vivian had been difficult, she'd been part of our wedding plans. I felt like I needed to show up for her.

Donnelly's was the only funeral home in Whitby. It was the kind of place that was small, very dignified, and smelled of furniture polish and lilies. The lighting was dim and respectful, and the carpet was thick enough to swallow footsteps. Soft classical music played from somewhere I couldn't identify.

When I walked in, I looked around in the dim lighting and saw a modest turnout. But after all, Vivian didn't have deep roots in the town. I recognized a few of the local vendors. There was a photographer I'd seen at local events and a woman who ran a rental company for wedding chairs and linens. Some couples who looked like they might have been former clients stood in small clusters, speaking in hushed voices. A few curious townspeople milled near the guest book. They were the kind who probably showed up at funerals whether they knew the deceased or not.

The casket was closed, which seemed fitting somehow. A large photograph of Vivian sat on an easel beside it. It was a professional headshot where Vivian looked polished and confident.

It was the Vivian who'd sold Grayson and me on her wedding planning services. Nothing like the woman I'd found at Jasper's farmhouse.

A man in a suit that was probably a bit too nice for Whitby stood near the guest book, accepting condolences. He had Vivian's coloring but a softer face. It must have been Vivian's brother. He looked a little younger than his sister and a little out of his depth. I spoke briefly to him, offered my sympathies, mentioned I'd been a client, then stepped aside.

Sarah Chen came in briefly to sign the book and pay her respects. She looked uncomfortable, like she wasn't sure she belonged there. She left quickly, giving me a quick wave and a smile as she went.

Tom Cross wasn't there at all. I wondered if it was too awkward for him, or if Vivian's brother simply hadn't mentioned the visitation to him.

Patricia Holbrook arrived and strode up to me after speaking with Vivian's brother. She was dressed appropriately in a navy dress and understated jewelry. "Ann. I thought I might see you here." She glanced around. "It's a smaller turnout than I expected." She was peering at the flower arrangements, tilting her head slightly. I had the uncomfortable feeling she was professionally evaluating them, even at a visitation.

"Vivian hasn't lived here as long as we have."

"True," said Patricia. She looked over with satisfaction at a spray of flowers nearby. "Ah. Glad to see my flowers arrived." Then she glanced around, lowering her voice slightly. "I suppose you've heard about Jasper."

I nodded.

"So tragic. Burton came to see me yesterday. I suppose he's talking to everyone again." She gave a slight eye-roll at the inconvenience of being questioned.

"I suppose he is."

Patricia said, "Of course, I didn't know anything about what happened. I was running errands very early. The dry cleaner, the post office. All my usual haunts."

It didn't sound like much of an alibi. In fact, it sounded like Patricia had been out and about and might have had the opportunity to zip over to the farmhouse.

Patricia glanced around the funeral home again. "I can't imagine all these people are genuinely grieving Vivian. I bet none of them were devastated by her death. I'm certainly not, and it would be dishonest to pretend I was. She did hurt my business. Actually, she hurt plenty of local businesses by hiring vendors elsewhere. But I am sorry she's dead."

"I'm sure Vivian's brother is glad we're here."

She nodded, still looking distracted. "Jasper is another matter entirely. He was one of the good ones. Of course, he and I were only business colleagues. However I still feel it's very sad."

I'd understood from Sarah that Patricia and Jasper had been close and that Patricia was very fond of him. I wondered if she was trying to create some distance there. She could be minimizing their connection to keep from looking suspiciously close to both murder victims.

I'd heard a lot about Vivian taking business away from Patricia. I had to wonder exactly what Patricia's financial situation was. I casually asked, "How's business going? It must be busy,

I'm guessing? Aren't there a good number of weddings near the holidays?"

"Oh, I'm doing fine. Yes, it's quite busy. After all, when you've been in this business as long as I have, you do build up a client base. Of course, Vivian took some of them, but I do have lots of repeat customers. They might start with a wedding, then have an anniversary party, or recommend me for a job-related event."

Her voice was confident and controlled. But then, business would surely be picking up now with Vivian gone.

"Besides, Vivian didn't work well with others, as I mentioned. By this point, my customers know I'm going to run their event without any drama. It wasn't the same with Vivian. The way she handled vendors was crazy. If one of them crossed her, she made sure he regretted it. I heard she got a photographer blacklisted from three venues."

"What?" I asked. "Why did she do that?"

"Because he had the nerve to push back on Vivian's timeline for the event. But I'm sure whoever murdered Vivian was probably closer to her. Not somebody upset about work stuff." Patricia glanced quickly around the funeral home for a minute. "You see Tom Cross isn't here. Vivian's ex."

"Maybe he thought it would attract attention away from remembering Vivian."

Patricia said, "Or maybe he's trying to lie low because he murdered Vivian."

Now I was the one looking around to make sure no one was listening in. "What makes you think that?"

"Tom had the most motive, right? He followed Vivian down here to Whitby, even though it meant giving up his job in Charlotte. Then he lost his job here."

I wasn't sure how Patricia knew all this. After all, Vivian had been telling everyone that she followed *him* to Whitby. But with a small town, people talked.

"Frankly, Tom's been behaving erratically ever since the divorce. He can't seem to find work. Half the time, he's at the park or on trails wandering around."

I said, "He's probably trying to stay busy. Or get exercise to help with stress."

Patricia sniffed. "Or else he's been thinking how Vivian is to blame for his entire situation. Which is the truth."

"But would Tom have murdered Jasper?"

"Sure he would, if he thought Jasper could implicate him in Vivian's murder. Maybe that's what happened," said Patricia.

"Did you know Jasper well?"

For a second, Patricia's throat worked hard, as if she were trying to repress a sob. Then she collected herself, her professional mask sliding back into place. "Well enough. He was a colleague, of course. We'd worked together on dozens of events over the years."

She smoothed her skirt, a gesture that seemed more about composing herself than fixing any wrinkle. "I was very impressed with him. He was always a hard worker and wanted everything to be perfect for the couples who hired him. Those biscuits of his?" She stopped, and for a moment I saw something real under the polish. It looked a little like genuine grief.

"He was impressive on the personal side of things, too," she continued, her voice steadier now.

"In what way?"

Patricia said, "Oh, he was always walking and trying to be careful about what he ate. Health-conscious, you know." She gave a small, sad smile. "I felt bad for him when I heard Vivian had been found at the farmhouse. That sort of thing couldn't have been good for business."

"No, I'd imagine not." I paused. "Can you think of anyone who might have wanted to hurt him?"

Patricia considered this. "Jasper knew everyone's business. He was at nearly every wedding or event. Maybe he knew or saw something he shouldn't have."

I raised my eyebrows. "So you think his death might be unconnected to Vivian's?"

She seemed to backpedal on this a little. "I'm not sure. That does seem a bit of a stretch, doesn't it? That would mean two murderers running around Whitby at once. Maybe Jasper knew who killed Vivian. That would be enough motive to murder him. Sarah Chen might have done it."

Patricia peered at me to make sure I was listening as she blamed my florist for Vivian's murder. Apparently, I locked attentive enough because she continued. "You know Sarah was pushing that local vendor coalition hard last year. She was trying to get all of us to band together into bundles because Vivian was outsourcing vendors from bigger cities."

Sarah, of course, had already told me about this. I had the feeling Patricia was about to mention the fact Jasper didn't want to be part of the bundle. But I wanted to hear what her spin on the situation was and how much it differed from Sarah's version.

"Jasper turned Sarah down," said Patricia with satisfaction. "He didn't want to rock the boat. It sounded like he preferred to work independently, too."

"Well, that's reasonable. He didn't want to do anything that would make him feel uncomfortable."

Patricia said, "Sarah didn't take it well, regardless. They were barely civil for months."

This was something Sarah hadn't mentioned. But maybe the rift wasn't as dramatic as Patricia was making it sound.

Patricia continued. "Sarah is struggling, truth be told. Her business simply isn't doing as well as it could be. And people can do desperate things when they're struggling."

I refrained from pointing out that Patricia's own business wasn't apparently doing as well as it might, either. For some reason, I felt somewhat defensive on Sarah's behalf. She seemed very much like an underdog to me, and I'd always had a soft spot for underdogs. I said, "I can't quite imagine Sarah attacking Jasper."

"I can't imagine why. He was clearly taken by surprise. And everyone knows he takes daily walks with those hand weights. He's been doing that forever. Rain or shine."

Clearly, this was something Patricia knew, too. "Those errands you mentioned that you ran after your client meeting. Did you happen to drive past the trail?"

There was just the slightest bit of hesitation, as if Patricia had been taken by surprise. "I don't even remember. I was in and out of businesses half the afternoon and had a lot on my mind."

She looked around. "I should mingle a little. Say hello to the Terrys. And Ann, if you need help with your wedding planning, remember I'm here. No pressure."

It felt like pressure, though. I reminded myself again to let Luna know what Mona might be in for if she talked with Patricia about planning.

I walked out to the parking lot, where I saw Burton leaning against his cruiser, watching people come and go. He looked as if he were working.

"Are you doing okay?" Burton asked. "You've had a crazy last week."

"I'm okay, thanks." I glanced back at the funeral home. "It was sort of unsettling being in there."

"I imagine so." He studied me for a moment. "Did you notice anything interesting inside?"

"I spoke with Patricia. She had a lot to say about other people's motives." I paused. "Tom Cross wasn't there."

Burton nodded. "He probably thought he'd be a distraction. And I don't think he and Vivian were on the best of terms at the end. I can see where he'd want to stay away." He pulled out a small notebook. "What did Patricia have to say?"

I filled him in as best I could, mentioning Patricia's weak alibi, her finger-pointing at Tom, and her sudden pivot to blaming Sarah. Burton took notes, his expression neutral. "So she's trying to throw everybody under the bus."

"It sounded that way. And Patricia didn't have much of an alibi for Jasper's death, which I'm sure you've already discovered."

Burton said, "She's not the only one with gaps in her morning." He didn't elaborate but moved on to another topic. "Have you remembered anything about your last conversation with Jasper at the library since we spoke?"

I shook my head. "No, that was really everything. The argument with the woman, the people hanging out and rubbernecking. He didn't say much else."

"Ok. You think of anything else, you give me a call."

Chapter Seventeen

Maybe I found talking to Patricia exhausting because all I could think about was heading home for a quick nap. I was ready to decompress with a certain cuddly orange cat. But when I pulled into my driveway, I spotted Zelda on the sidewalk, obviously waiting for me.

"There you are. I was starting to think you'd moved out and not told anyone."

Zelda wasn't one for friendly preambles. I hoped she wasn't waiting for me to push for the HOA architectural review of the addition. Or, actually, *anything* HOA-related. I wasn't feeling quite up to it.

"Is everything okay?" I walked over to join her on the sidewalk, hoping our conversation could be conducted entirely outside.

"I've had three neighbors ask me when your construction is wrapping up. The Kennellys want to know about the trucks. The Greers are convinced the noise is affecting her blood pressure. And Bill Weaver has created some sort of countdown calendar."

I said rather wearily, "Honestly, I don't know the exact timeline. The contractor says it could be on track to be done by the wedding, but you know how that goes."

"I do know. Which is why I told them all to be patient and mind their own business."

I blinked at her. I'd expected a complaint and instead got Zelda running interference. "Thanks, Zelda. I appreciate that."

Zelda waved it off. "It's a construction project. People need perspective. Or a life." Then she eyed my outfit. "You're dressed up for your off-day. Did you get called into work?"

"I was at the visitation for Vivian."

Zelda sniffed. "How was the visitation? Who was the one who organized it?"

"Her brother came in from the west coast."

Zelda leaned in curiously. "Were there many people there?"

"No, she might not have had a lot of close friends here. I'd say the people attending were mostly business acquaintances."

Zelda nodded. "I can't say I'm surprised. I heard plenty about Vivian. The woman acted like Whitby was some backwater town. Like she was doing us all a favor by gracing us with her presence. Was the visitation at her house?"

"No, it was at the funeral home."

Zelda sniffed again. "Donnelly's has really gone downhill. It used to be dignified. Now they've got those fake electric candles everywhere. They look like a restaurant that's trying too hard. Everything's going to the dogs. Even funeral homes." She peered more closely at me. "You look tired."

And getting wearier by the second. "It's been a long week."

"Are you eating enough?" demanded Zelda. "You can't run on fumes."

Before I could answer, Zelda continued, "I make a mean chicken and dumplings. It's a prized old family recipe. I could bring some by."

I felt touched. To my aggravation, I felt my eyes prickling with tears. I nodded wordlessly.

Zelda growled, "Don't make it into a thing. It's just food."

I noticed Zelda was fidgeting, her fingers tapping against her arm. "How's the non-smoking going?"

"Still not smoking. Still want to murder someone." She paused, realizing what she said. "Scratch that. Poor choice of words. Anyway, the sunflower seeds I chew definitely help with my cravings. But I gave myself a canker sore last week from eating too many. At least my lungs are clear. I suppose."

"That's awesome, Zelda, really."

"It's stupid, that's what it is. I've exposed everyone to decades of secondhand smoke, and now I'm trying to save myself. I should have quit twenty years ago." But there was a flicker of pride under the gruffness.

Then she glanced around at the quiet street. "I've been keeping my eyes open with everything going on. You notice things when you're walking the neighborhood instead of ducking out for smoke breaks."

"You mean you've been doing a neighborhood watch walk because of the murders?"

Zelda gave me a scornful look. "I'm *always* doing a neighborhood watch walk. But I've been stepping it up. But it's not just extended to our neighborhood. I'm keeping my eyes open on the way to the shop and back."

Besides volunteering at the library, Zelda also worked as a receptionist/admin at the local auto-body shop. "Have you noticed anything odd during your commutes?"

"That ex-husband of Vivian's has been over at that trail by the caterer's farmhouse a couple of times this past week."

Tom Cross. Sarah Chen had mentioned seeing him near the trail, too. I said, "He might be exercising. He was telling me he was trying to stay fit."

"That would involve him getting out of his car. When I've spotted him, he's just been sitting there. Not getting out, not walking or jogging or whatnot. Sitting."

I said slowly, "Maybe he's grieving Vivian in his own way. She was found at the farmhouse, you know."

"Or maybe he's remembering how he killed her there. And Jasper, too." Zelda pursed her lips. "I'm not saying he did anything, mind you. I'm just saying it's odd behavior. And I notice odd behavior."

Before I could reply, Zelda waved her hand at the house. "Are you and Grayson still getting married? With all this chaos?"

I was starting to think I should have invited Zelda inside. My exhaustion was catching up with me, and I shifted on my feet. "Of course."

Zelda gave a curt nod. "Okay. I can help you out if you need it. Everything seems to be a disaster. Your cottage is under construction. Your wedding planner and your caterer are dead. And a killer's loose in Whitby. There's a lot going on."

"Thanks, Zelda. We're keeping everything simple. I'm hoping the construction stuff will be mostly done with for the wedding. And we'll figure out the food." I realized I hadn't really even talked to Grayson about what our backup plan was.

"You should do a potluck," growled Zelda. "Tell everyone BYOF."

"BYOF?"

"Bring your own food. You're smart to keep it all simple. None of that fussy nonsense. Your great-aunt would have approved."

This made me smile. I was never sure how Zelda felt about my great-aunt, who'd raised me in this very cottage. They were both two strong-willed women, so maybe they hadn't gotten along as well as they might have. But I appreciated her saying she'd have approved. I said so.

Zelda said dismissively, "It's the truth. You're doing everything right. Listen, I married an idiot when I was young. I thought I knew what I was doing, but I didn't. It lasted four years, but it felt like forty."

I'd never heard her mention a husband before. "I'm sorry, Zelda."

"Ancient history. The point is, I know the difference between a poor match and a good one." She looked directly at me. "Grayson's ten times the man my ex was. You picked well." She said it as if she were delivering a verdict, not a compliment.

"Thank you."

She immediately deflected. "Don't thank me. I'm only stating facts." She checked her watch. "I've got to get back. My soap opera's on in a few minutes, and I refuse to miss Janelle marrying Scott because of small talk." She turned to leave, but then turned back around. "If you need anything, you know where I am. Don't be a stranger."

It was delivered almost like a threat, but I knew better.

I did end up taking a nap. Actually, it was a glorious nap. And I did it properly. I got into bed, pulled the soft quilt up to my chin, put on my eye mask to keep the light out, and curled up with Fitz. His contented purr was the last thing I heard before I drifted off. What's more, I only slept for forty-five minutes, which was both long enough to revive me and short enough that I shouldn't have a problem falling asleep that night.

After I'd had something to eat, I gave Luna a call. Seeing Patricia again today had reminded me I wanted to give her a friendly heads-up about her mom's interest in engaging Patricia for wedding planning. I knew Luna was working, so I texted first to ask her to call me when she was on break. She phoned me right away.

"The whole day is a break," she told me. "Nobody's here at the library for some reason."

"It's funny how it's never really like that when I'm there."

Luna said, "Right? It's always slammed and crazy when you're here. So maybe you need to stay home more," she said with a chuckle. "Well, you clearly survived Vivian's visitation. How was it?"

"It was fine. Kind of a small turnout, but that's what I was expecting. Patricia Holbrook was working the room like it was a networking event."

"Classy," said Luna.

"Speaking of Patricia, I wanted to give you a heads-up. She and your mom talked at the library last week. It sounded like Mona might be considering using her for the wedding."

Luna said, "Ugh. I thought we had it covered. I was helping out Mom and Wilson with the planning and phone calls and stuff. I think Mom just wants to abdicate responsibility for the thing. She's not the most patient person in the world."

"Really? She knits. I thought knitters were all patient."

"A common misconception," said Luna breezily. "Anyway, thanks for letting me know. I'll try to get ahead of that. We've got some plans hammered out, and I'd hate it if Patricia came in and started changing everything."

"Patricia seems pretty persistent. Probably because there are business opportunities now that Vivian is out of the picture."

Luna said, "I can't really tell Mom who to hire, but it really is annoying."

"How is everything else going? How are you and Jeremy? The flowers seemed like an apology to me."

Her voice sounded a little lighter. "They were. Jeremy felt awful that he didn't realize how self-centered he'd come across. I told him I didn't mean for him to give up on a great opportunity."

"What did he say to that?"

I could tell she was smiling on the other end. "He said he didn't want to give up on a great relationship, either. Jeremy wanted to see if he could have both things. Greedy of him." But she sounded pleased.

"Has he heard back on the remote work?"

Luna said, "Not yet. He's trying not to pester the guy, but I can tell he's anxious. He keeps checking his phone when we're together." She paused. "And I keep pretending I'm not watching him check it."

"That sounds a little stressful."

"It is. But Jeremy's annoyingly upbeat about the whole thing. He keeps saying it'll work out one way or another." Luna didn't sound annoyed, though. She sounded fond. "Tonight, we're going to drink wine and watch a really terrible reality show. Self-care, you know."

"That sounds like a solid plan."

"You should try it sometime," said Luna. "Instead of, you know, attending funerals and interrogating suspects."

"I wouldn't say I was interrogating anyone."

"Mmm." Then she changed course. "Hey, what about the wedding? I'm really sorry about everything. Vivian, Jasper, the construction."

"It's a lot. But Grayson's been awesome. The wedding's still on, although it might be dramatically changing. Zelda offered me chicken and dumplings in commiseration."

"Zelda?" asked Luna. "Voluntarily offering food? The apocalypse really is upon us."

I laughed.

"Okay, I'd better run. A mom is coming into the children's area with a kid in tow. Talk to you later."

Chapter Eighteen

The next morning I was back at the library. Sunlight streamed through the tall windows, catching dust motes in the air and warming the reading nooks. I'd just finished up some reference work when I saw Tom Cross over at the small bank of public computers near the reference section. There were four terminals, usually occupied by job seekers, seniors checking email, and teens playing games. Tom was looking more rumpled than ever. His tired eyes were deeper-set, and he was wearing a button-down that had seen better days. He was typing slowly, occasionally stopping to stare at the screen.

I walked over and paused at his terminal. Tom glanced up. "Ann," he said, looking a bit bemused. "I didn't expect to see you here."

"I work here," I said with a smile.

"Right. Of course you do." He ran a hand through his hair, making it look even worse than it had before. "My laptop is on the blink. I think it's the charging port. Anyway, I needed to fill out some job applications." He gestured to the library computer. "Public resources."

"That's what they're there for," I said. "How's the job search coming along?"

Tom shook his head. "It's not going great, especially locally. I've extended it to Charlotte, but it's looking like the market isn't very solid right now." He made a face and lowered his voice. "And locally, I'm still a suspect in a murder case, so that doesn't help. Or more than one murder case. You heard what happened to Jasper Webb."

I nodded.

Tom rubbed his face with one hand, looking exhausted. "I really didn't know him very well, although I met him a few times when Vivian and I were still together. He catered some of her events. I don't think she gave him the praise he deserved for those. From what I've heard, Jasper did a fantastic job in his niche."

"His niche?"

"Southern food. Especially barbeque. Vivian tended to want something more formal at her weddings, but there's something to be said for comfort food. It just makes people happy. And isn't that what you want at a wedding?"

I said, "What did you make of Jasper?"

"He seemed like a good guy. He was the kind of person who actually remembered your name and asked how you were doing. And Jasper was pretty laid-back." Tom chuckled. "Laid-back was the opposite of Vivian, which I'm sure drove her nuts."

"You mentioned you're a suspect in his murder?" I asked.

He looked even wearier than before, if that was possible. "Yeah, I guess so. I mean, if I'm a suspect for Vivian's, wouldn't they apply that to Jasper's as well? Even though I didn't really even know him. Of course, I didn't have an alibi, either. Being jobless isn't helping me out on that score. Although I was at the gym."

"Isn't being at the gym an alibi?"

He gave me a rueful look. "I was just one of a slew of people over there. They were having a free trial day. I figured I'd take advantage of it since my gym membership was one of the first things I cut out after the divorce. But it's not like the fitness center was taking attendance over there. I showed up, did some time on the treadmill and with the weights, then I left. No one was keeping track of when I showed up or headed out."

"I'm sure most people don't have witnesses to what they were doing."

Tom said, "I only wish I knew when these murders were going to happen so I could make sure I did. I make a very convenient suspect."

"When we were talking at the park, you mentioned Vivian leaving behind a bunch of unhappy brides. Were you able to point the police to anyone in particular?"

Tom thought for a minute. "Well, I couldn't seem to summon up the name on demand when they were asking me. But there was one name that came to mind. Her name was Jessica something, I think."

"Jessica Morton?"

"That's right," said Tom. "It was a disaster. I mean, everything fell apart. The flowers were wrong, the cake was a mess, the photographer had some kind of scheduling mix-up. Vivian came home from it looking like she'd been through a war. She was stressed about it for weeks."

"What happened to the bride?"

Tom's expression was grim. "She was furious. She tried to get refunds, said she was going to sue us . . . all kinds of stuff."

"*Was* she going to sue?"

Tom said, "Who knows? She didn't seem to have much income, but a lawyer might have been willing to take her on if he thought she could win. But it never happened. Although she wrote a ton of bad reviews all over the place." He shrugged. "I mean, I get it. Your wedding day is supposed to be this perfect day. When it's ruined, it's tough to forget about it. Have you ever talked to Jessica?"

I nodded.

Tom shook his head. "I ran into her husband at Quittin' Time a couple of months back. Ex-husband now, I guess. We ended up sitting next to each other at the bar there. Two guys whose marriages didn't survive Vivian Cross." He gave a humorless laugh. "He told me the wedding day broke them. That Jessica couldn't let it go, but kept replaying every detail, over and over. He finally just left and got an annulment."

I thought about Jessica's carefully controlled smile and the way she'd turned away when Grayson asked about her marriage. She's said something about how they're working through things.

"That's sad," I said.

"It is. It really is. He said she was stuck. Like Jessica couldn't move forward until someone paid for what happened."

I was quiet for a few moments. "Is there anyone you can think of who'd have wanted to hurt Jasper? I don't suppose Jessica would have had a motive to murder him."

"That's what I can't figure out. I mean, with Vivian. I could make a list of people who might have had it in for her. She tended to make enemies everywhere she went. But Jasper was a nice guy. It's hard to picture someone having a grudge against him." He frowned. "Although I guess he might have known something. Vivian was found at his farmhouse, after all. Maybe Jasper saw someone coming or going." He shook his head, unwilling to speculate further.

I said after a moment, "Do you mind if I ask you something? You and Vivian sounded like you were together for a long time. What was she like before everything fell apart?"

Tom was quiet for a few moments. When he finally spoke, his voice was softer. "Assured. That's what I fell in love with. Vivian always knew exactly what she wanted. When we first met, she was planning weddings out of her apartment, talking about them like she was orchestrating royal events or state dinners or something. She made everything and everyone feel important." He gave a sad smile. "She made me feel important, too, for a while."

Tom seemed lost in memories, so I stayed silent, waiting for him to continue.

"We took this trip to the coast, early on. Vivian carefully planned out every detail. I mean, not just where we were staying. The restaurants we should eat at, the timing of the tides and the sunsets, so we could take pictures, all that kind of stuff. Most people would find that kind of planning exhausting, but back then, it felt like I was being taken care of. Like someone else was handling all the hard parts."

I said, "I can definitely see the appeal in that. It's nice not having to make decisions all the time, isn't it?" That was exactly the reason Grayson and I had hired Vivian to begin with. She was so confident and experienced. It felt like we could hand everything off to her, simply show up for our wedding, and have an amazing, easy day.

"Sure. Making lots of decisions can be stressful, right? But for Vivian, she had this underlying need to control everything. And that control was what made our marriage fall apart. I just didn't see it until I was on the wrong side of it."

"One thing that's been confusing for me," I said slowly. "Vivian was obviously such a perfectionist. Such a control freak, as you're saying. But then I hear about these weddings that went really wrong; the Morrison wedding in Charlotte, for one. And Jessica Morton's wedding here in Whitby. Then you've mentioned a string of unhappy brides. How does someone so obsessed with control have events fall apart like that?"

Tom leaned back in his chair, considering this. "The Morrison wedding was a perfect storm. The mother of the bride even had a medical emergency. A surprise rainstorm popped up. There was a lot of stuff that went wrong that even the best planning wouldn't have been able to prevent. It wasn't that Vivian didn't plan; she planned obsessively. But she couldn't *adapt*. When things went sideways, she froze up instead of being flexible. Her whole system depended on everything going exactly right. When it didn't, she had no backup mode."

"So the need for control was actually the root of the problem."

"Right," Tom said. "Most planners would have improvised. They'd have moved the ceremony inside, reshuffled the timeline, done whatever it took. Vivian simply couldn't. It was like watching a computer crash. That's what really destroyed her reputation in Charlotte. It wasn't so much that things went wrong. I mean, stuff probably goes wrong at almost every wedding. It was more that she fell apart and then blamed everyone else afterward."

"And Jessica's wedding?"

Tom's expression shifted into a grimace. "I don't know all the details, but from what Vivian told me, the flowers were a shade off from what the bride wanted. The cake was late. Not hours late, but maybe forty-five minutes. There was some sort of tension with the photographer. Maybe there were some brides who could have laughed about it later."

"But Jessica didn't."

"Nope," said Tom. "And Vivian made it worse. She was always awful at apologizing. I guess she never liked claiming fault. It was that way in our marriage, too, unfortunately. Anyway, when Jessica complained about what happened, Vivian became defensive and dismissive. She practically blamed Jessica for the issues because the wedding was fairly low-budget."

I nodded. "That's probably the worst thing to say to an upset bride."

"Exactly. Jessica was already pretty fragile about the whole thing, then Vivian was basically telling her she was being unreasonable for asking for perfection when she hadn't paid for perfection." Tom looked uncomfortable. "I'm not trying to excuse Vivian in any way. But Jessica's version of what happened and the reality were pretty far apart. She'd convinced herself her whole day was ruined. And that Vivian had deliberately sabotaged her."

I thought about Jessica's precise recollections of every detail. She'd talked about neon fuchsia flowers and a photographer argument that lasted half the reception.

Tom said, "You know, some people kind of hold onto things, especially when they feel like they've been wronged." He gave a short laugh. Vivian seemed to have a gift for making people feel wronged."

I looked back over at the computer where Tom had an application up. "It's got to be hard being in Whitby right now. Do you have any family nearby? Someone to lean on for support?"

Tom's expression tightened. "My dad's in Raleigh. He's a retired surgeon there. Dad keeps calling to check in, which is his way of finding out whether I've been arrested yet." His laugh was hollow. "Here I am, unemployed, divorced, and suspected of murdering my ex-wife. I'm not exactly the family legacy he had in mind."

I was quiet again, waiting.

Tom continued. "He wanted me to be a doctor and follow in his footsteps. Instead, I followed Vivian to a small town and lost everything." He looked over at me. "It would help if I could get in front of any kind of allegation. I always feel like I'm blindsided whenever I talk with the cops. Have you heard anyone talking about me?"

I thought about Sarah Chen and Zelda seeing Tom near the trail. I said, "I did hear you were parked near the trail by

Jasper's farmhouse. That it might have been around the time Jasper died."

"Oh man. I know how it looks, believe me. But I was only there to get on the trail. Working out has been my only form of stress relief lately."

I said slowly, "But you mentioned you were at the gym for the free trial day. Did you need to get more exercise after that?"

He was very still. After a few beats, he said, "Okay. I didn't want to say why I was over there because it makes me look like this kind of sad person. Vivian was found at the farmhouse. I felt like I needed to go over there and think. Process all this It's not like I can visit her grave because there isn't one yet. Her brother's handling everything, and he's made it clear he doesn't want me to be involved." Tom swallowed. "So I sat in my car like an idiot and thought about the woman I used to love. That's the big suspicious behavior everyone's talking about."

"You weren't at the visitation. Did Vivian's brother prevent you from going?"

Tom's laugh was bitter. "No, but I couldn't face a roomful of people who thought I killed her. They'd all be watching to see if I'd slip up or confess or cry the wrong way." He shook his head. "I know avoiding it probably made me look even more guilty. But I couldn't do it." He shrugged. "Anyway, I'd probably have been distracting if I'd been there. And the visitation was supposed to be about Vivian."

I said, "Going back to the job search. Where are you planning to proceed from here? Are you looking at expanding your search? I know you mentioned the job market not being strong right now."

"I'll go wherever I can find something. I'm not in the position to be picky. I have a few things in the pipeline."

"Things in the pipeline" was often something I heard when there was nothing in the pipeline at all. "Hey, if you need help with the job search, come by the reference desk. We have some databases that might be useful for you. ReferenceUSA has business listings and company profiles, which might be helpful if you're researching potential employers. And I've got resume software if you need to update yours."

Tom looked surprised, then grateful. "I hadn't thought about the library for that kind of thing."

"Most people don't. There are other things that might help, too. You've mentioned you were in banking. Sometimes bankers go into consulting or go independent when corporate jobs dry up. We can connect you with SCORE. They do free mentorship for people starting businesses. A lot of retired executives work with them."

Tom nodded slowly. "I've thought about hanging out my own shingle sometimes. Maybe financial advising? I'm just not sure where to start."

"That's exactly what SCORE is for. Come by when you're ready, and I'll help you get set up."

"Thanks, Ann." He gave me a small, tired smile. "You're the first person who's offered to help."

"That's what I'm here for."

Chapter Nineteen

Tom did a little more work on applications, then came up to the reference desk to get started finding out more about advising. He ended up leaving the library looking more confident than he had before.

The interaction I had with Tom left me feeling unexpectedly sympathetic toward him. I decided to run it by Grayson later. For now, I surveyed the library. I took in the quiet hum of the afternoon, a few patrons browsing the stacks, and the soft click of keyboards from the computer section. I saw Linus had set up at one of the tables near the windows. The chessboard was out, and Timothy was sitting across from him. Owen watched intently from a nearby chair. Making the tableau complete, Zelda was shelving books nearby, casting occasional glances at the game.

I walked over to join them. Timothy seemed to be thinking hard, his hand hovering over a knight.

"Who's winning?" I asked.

Linus straightened his glasses. "The outcome isn't yet determined. Though Timothy's position has perhaps narrowed a bit."

Timothy gave me a rueful look. "He means I'm about to lose again. But I'm learning."

"Timothy lasted way longer this time. Last week, Linus beat him in like twelve moves," said Owen.

Timothy grinned at him. "Thanks for the support, Owen."

"I mean it! You're getting better."

Timothy made a move, and Linus studied the board.

"Interesting choice," said Linus. "You're protecting your bishop but exposing your rook. Why?"

"I thought you were going to—" Timothy stopped. "Oh, wait. You wanted me to think that."

Owen said, "Very tricky, Mr. Truman!"

Before Linus could make another move on the board, I saw Mrs. Sullivan enter the library, and groaned internally. She spotted me immediately and approached with purpose.

"Ann! Just the person I wanted to see."

I braced myself for another two-factor crisis.

"I wanted to let you know I've successfully logged into my bank account four times this week. Without a single issue."

I felt a wave of relief wash over me. "That's fantastic, Mrs. Sullivan."

"Like you said, it's all about the correct text message order. It's so completely counterintuitive, of course. The system is still quite fundamentally flawed. But I've managed to adapt."

I said, "I'm glad it's working for you."

She leaned in conspiratorially. "I've been telling everyone. Edna Morrow has had the same problem. She didn't know about the bottom message being the most recent, either. I straightened her out."

"Good for you! You're becoming a resource."

Mrs. Sullivan said, "Someone has to. The banks certainly aren't going to explain this properly. And I've told everyone that, if they run into a problem they can't fix, Ann Beckett at the library can help them."

Timothy, overhearing, gave me a wry look. I quickly said, "Actually, we have a monthly tech day where we encourage patrons to come in with their devices. We offer advice there to help with any issues they have. Of course, coming in at other times is fine, too."

But Mrs. Sullivan's attention was already being drawn in another direction. "What's all this?"

"Chess club," said Timothy. "Sort of, anyway. It's informal."

She studied the board. "I used to play, you know. My husband taught me. He was quite good."

Linus cleared his throat. "Would you care to join us sometime?"

Mrs. Sullivan looked surprised, then pleased. "I haven't played in years. I'd probably be terrible. Actually, I *know* I'd be terrible."

Owen said, "You'd get better with practice, though. You could relearn it with me. It would be fun to have somebody more at my level."

She considered this, the look of surprise turning into a smile. "Perhaps. I'll think about it." She nodded crisply and headed toward the periodicals, but there was a slight spring to her step.

Zelda, finished with her shelving, walked over to us. "I bet she'll do it. Jan Sullivan doesn't turn down a challenge."

"You know her?" I asked.

"Sure do. She ran the most successful real estate office in town for thirty years. She didn't get that kind of success by backing down from competition."

Linus nodded. "Good point."

Fitz, who'd been lying in a nearby sunbeam, stretched, yawned, and relocated closer to us.

"I think Fitz wants to cheer us on," said Linus. "Owen, do you want to play? Maybe with Timothy?"

As I headed to the reference desk, Owen and Timothy were facing off across the chessboard with Fitz watching the proceedings with interest.

I spent a little time at the circulation desk to fill in for a library tech. Luna, who was working an afternoon shift, came in with her mom. She gave me a quick nod and headed for the children's section for an impending storytime, and Mona walked over to talk to me at the desk.

"Hey there, Mona," I said.

She beamed at me. "It's good to see you, Ann. I've been meaning to call you and thank you for joining Wilson and me at the trail. That was so kind of you. I'm sorry I interrupted your quiet time like that. We were so flabbergasted and the first thing I could think of was calling you. Luna was working, of course."

"I was glad you called me, Mona. I'm just sorry you had to find Jasper like that." I glanced over at Wilson, who was still scowling at his computer screen as he had been all morning. "Wilson's been burying himself at work when I've been at the library. He hasn't been out of his office much."

Mona nodded. "That's exactly what I was hoping to talk to you about. It was very distressing to Wilson. I mean, it was distressing to me, too, but finding Jasper really did affect him badly."

"We probably need to get him out of the library and distract him."

"That's what I was thinking, too," said Mona. "The birdwatching was such a great activity for us. It's been something active we can do together. You know how I was when you first met me."

I did. Mona had knee replacement surgery, and the resulting lack of mobility had triggered a deep depression. That's why she and Luna were living together; she'd asked Luna to move back home from New York to help with her recovery. Mona struggled with PT exercises and even the motivation to get out of bed and get dressed. She was so much better now than she'd been then. "I sure do."

"Wilson's clearly not going to take up knitting, and he's not going to play the video games Jeremy and I play together. The birdwatching fit the bill as our couple's activity. I really don't want him to give up on it because of what happened. But I know I can't push him too hard." She paused, giving me a sweetly beseeching look. "I was thinking if you came back to the trail with us tomorrow morning, it might help. It would simply be a group outing, instead of the two of us. Are you available tomorrow?"

I nodded. "I'm not working, and I could probably use the fresh air, myself. What time were you thinking?"

We set up the details, then started chatting about other things. Mona brought up weddings, which was where most of our conversations tended to end up, no matter how they'd started. "By the way, Wilson and I made a decision about the wedding planning. Remember when you and I talked to the planner before book club?"

I nodded.

"Luna mentioned Patricia was a bit bossy." Mona smiled. "That might be fine for some people. But Wilson and I don't really need anyone managing us. We've been managing our personal things our whole lives. I've made some good inroads with planning in the last few days. At first, all the different options were rather off-putting. But I feel like it's more under-control now. Simple, pretty, no fuss."

"That sounds perfect for you two."

A patron walked up, and Mona quickly repeated the details for tomorrow morning. "See you then. I'm hoping to spot that pileated woodpecker finally. Wilson's sworn he's been hearing it for weeks, but we can't spot him."

Later that afternoon, I took a break from research to walk over to the reading area where Linus and Zelda were playing chess. And bickering. Zelda, although she claimed to be rusty, had walked over and challenged Linus to a game. From what I understood, Linus's friend Harold was still recovering from his fall and wasn't up for playing chess yet.

"Are you going to move sometime this century?" grated Zelda.

"Chess requires contemplation. It's not checkers."

Zelda groused, "At this rate, I'll have taken up smoking and quit again before you make a move."

I smiled at them. "How's the game going?"

"Slowly. Very slowly," said Zelda.

Linus said with dignity, "I'm considering all my options."

From what I could see, Zelda appeared to be losing, despite her impatience to continue the game.

"How are things going with Ivy?" I asked Linus.

"Wonderful," said Linus, sounding pleased. "I bought her a dog bed, as you suggested. I purchased one of those orthopedic ones, since she's not a particularly young dog. She's a smart girl, you know. Ivy took to it right away."

Zelda looked up from the chessboard. "You bought your dog an orthopedic bed?"

"She has joint issues," Linus said with dignity.

"My back has joint issues. I don't have an orthopedic bed."

"Perhaps you should consider one," Linus suggested mildly.

Zelda glowered at the chessboard.

He peered at the chessboard. "I suppose a move is necessary. Ivy is waiting at home for her afternoon walk."

I said, "Ivy's such a good girl. And a smart one."

Linus smiled. "She sure is. She knows my schedule even better than I do. She'll be at the door with her leash."

"Dogs are better than people," Zelda said with certainty. "Present company excluded. Maybe."

"I'll take 'maybe' as a compliment," said Linus. He finally made his move. It was a good one, putting Zelda in quite the awkward position.

She stared at the board, then at Linus. "You were stalling on purpose. You knew exactly what you were going to do."

Linus looked quite innocent. "I was contemplating."

"You're a menace, Linus." But there was grudging respect in her voice.

I left them to it, smiling as I walked away. The library was starting to hum with quiet activity. Wilson passed Zelda and Linus, pausing to watch their game for a few moments and commiserate with Zelda.

Chapter Twenty

At 5:00, my shift ended, so I texted Grayson to see if he might want to go to Quittin' Time for supper. He accepted quickly, and I told him I'd walk over to the newspaper office.

The Whitby Times occupied a modest storefront on Main Street. It was a narrow building squeezed between a boutique and a long-closed hardware store. Inside were a few desks cluttered with notebooks and coffee cups, and the hum of an ancient air conditioning unit, which was running despite the cooler temps outside. The space smelled of newsprint and old coffee.

Grayson looked up with a grin when I walked in. He was talking on his cell phone and jotting down notes. He motioned for me to join him in the glass-enclosed office at the back of the large newsroom.

He wrapped up his phone conversation, then gave me a hug. "Ready to head out to supper?"

"Actually, I am. For some reason, I'm starving tonight. I did eat lunch."

He said, "I'm pretty hungry, too. Maybe we could both use protein."

We were about to head out when the door to the newsroom opened. Jessica Morton walked in.

"Ann," she said. "I didn't realize you'd be here."

"I just dropped by," I said.

"Well, it's good to see you." She paused. "Is this a bad time? I wanted to bounce something off you, Grayson."

He gave me a quick look, then said, "No, this is fine."

"Should I step out?" I asked.

Jessica shook her head. "No, no. You can stick around. It's nothing private." Her gaze switched over to Grayson. "I wanted to talk with you about the newspaper coverage of Vivian Cross."

"What about the coverage?" Grayson's voice was professional, but guarded.

She took a deep breath. "I just wanted to make sure it was balanced. You know. I talked about that during our first visit at my house. I want to make sure the newspaper isn't running a profile about Vivian that overlooks the negative parts of her personality. People need to understand exactly who Vivian really was."

Jessica seemed nervous as she twisted one of her bracelets on her arm. "I've seen how this kind of thing usually goes. Someone dies, and suddenly they're a saint. All the bad things they've done get erased. Vivian was no saint. I don't want people to forget that."

Grayson said in a measured tone, "I don't usually write puff pieces. I cover the facts."

"The facts, sure. But facts can be framed in different ways, can't they?" She leaned forward, her expression more pleading than accusatory. "I'm a great example of what Vivian did to people. She messed up their lives. And now everyone's acting like she was this successful businesswoman who died this tragic death. They're not talking about all the bad things she did."

I could hear the anger beneath her words. And nervous energy radiated from her.

Then Jessica frowned. She glanced between Grayson and me. "Wait. Are you two an item? Were you Vivian's clients?"

"She was planning our wedding, yes," I said.

Her eyes widened slightly. "You didn't mention that when we talked before."

Grayson said, "It didn't really seem relevant."

Jessica was quiet for a moment. Then she let out a breath that was almost a laugh. "Then you totally understand. You know exactly what she was like." She leaned forward again, as if she'd found an ally. "You understand the way Vivian pushed and pushed. She always made people feel like nothing they wanted was good enough. It was almost like your own wedding wasn't really yours anymore, it was hers."

It was clear Jessica thought she'd found common ground as she continued. "She did that to everyone, you know. Vivian liked to make people think their taste was awful and your choices were all wrong. Like you should be grateful she was there to fix everything."

She wasn't wrong. I gave a slight nod of my head. Letting her talk might be the best way to get more information.

Jessica continued, "I tried so hard to make my wedding exactly what I wanted. All I was looking for was simple and meaningful. Blush and ivory. Garden roses. A string quartet for the ceremony, not a DJ. I had Pinterest boards for everything and knew exactly what I wanted."

Her voice had taken on a rehearsed quality, as if she'd told this story many times before to friends, therapists, and to herself in the mirror. "And Vivian turned it into a disaster. I told you both what happened. Everything fell apart, and she stood there with her clipboard, acting like it was everybody else's fault. The flowers were fuchsia. Fuchsia." She said the word as if it were a crime. "I can still picture them. Neon pink against the ivory linens I'd spent three months choosing. It was like a joke, you know? Like someone was playing a joke on me."

Grayson caught my eye. I wasn't sure what he was thinking, but I knew what I was thinking. This was a woman who hadn't moved on. Not even a little.

Grayson said, "I'm really sorry that happened to you."

Jessica said, "All any bride wants is her perfect day. That's not too much to ask, is it? Just one perfect day."

Grayson said, "Did you hear about Jasper's death?"

Jessica's eyes clouded. "Yes. Jasper was one of the good ones. He really was." Her voice softened. "I hated that Vivian used outside caterers instead of him. Jasper deserved better than that. I can't believe someone would hurt him. He was sweet, you know? The kind of guy who always remembered your name and asked how your day was going."

Grayson said, "You haven't heard anything about anyone who might have wished him harm?"

Jessica was quiet for a moment. "I keep thinking about Vivian's ex-husband, Tom." She lowered her voice slightly, as if she were sharing something delicate. "I heard he was so angry during the divorce. Maybe that anger built up, and he lost control one day. It can happen. Then, what if Jasper realized Tom killed Vivian? Maybe Tom figured out that Jasper knew he'd done it. Wouldn't Tom want to kill Jasper, too?" She looked at Grayson. "Are you in contact with the police? Do they have any leads?"

"It sounds like they're pursuing multiple leads," he said non-committally.

"Of course," she said nodding. "I'm sure they are. "But they need to figure out who's behind this. Two people are dead. Who knows when the killer might stop?"

Grayson said, "The police seemed to be following up with people they'd spoken to before. Have they reached out to you at all?"

"They did. They explained it was all routine. Naturally, they asked where I was when Jasper was murdered, although it didn't sound like they had much of a handle as to when that was. I told them I'd done my customer service shift early, then ran out to the grocery store to pick up a few things." She shrugged. "Not much of an alibi, I guess."

Jessica gave us a tight smile. "Anyway, I'm sorry I held you up. Like I said, I don't want Vivian to be remembered like some kind of hero. She ruined events for people. Your wedding day is supposed to be the happiest day of your life." Her smile softened as she looked at me. "I hope your wedding is everything you want it to be. I really do. You deserve your perfect day."

Then she headed out, the door chiming as it closed behind her.

"That was . . . something," Grayson said slowly.

"It's kind of sad," I said. "Jessica is really stuck in the past with her wedding. She's never moved past it."

My stomach growled loudly, and we both laughed. "I think it's time for us to head over to Quittin' Time before someone else drops by the newsroom," Grayson said.

He locked up the office, and we walked the few blocks over. The evening air had an early-October crispness to it, and the streetlights were flickering on along Main Street.

Quittin' Time was a family-owned restaurant in its third generation. The linoleum on the floors had seen better days, and the vinyl covering the booths was torn in spots, but the place was always immaculately clean and the service was prompt and friendly. The hostess settled us into a booth near the window and handed us the old laminated menus. I already knew what I wanted, though: meatloaf with mashed potatoes and green beans. It was the kind of comfort food that made everything feel fixable, at least temporarily.

Grayson ordered the fried catfish with coleslaw and hush puppies. When the waitress brought out sweet teas, we chatted for a few minutes about inconsequential things, just enjoying being together.

But I couldn't keep my mind totally off of everything that had happened. No matter what subjects we tried to discuss, my thoughts kept drifting back to the investigation. Fortunately, Grayson understood. "Okay," he said. "Let's sort through what we've got."

I nodded. It really helped to lay it all out, even if we didn't have answers yet.

"There's Tom Cross, Vivian's ex. He's bitter about the divorce, struggling financially, and lost his job moving to Whitby to help out Vivian's career."

"Right," I said. "He was also spotted sitting in his truck near the farmhouse by Zelda and Sarah Chen. I actually spoke with Tom today when he came by the library to use the computer for job applications."

Grayson raised his eyebrows. "How was he?"

"Tom seemed tired to me. I didn't really get any angry vibe from him." I took a sip of my tea. "He said he was sitting near the farmhouse because he couldn't visit Vivian's grave. Basically, being close to where she died was how he grieved."

Grayson was quiet for a moment. "That's either very sad or an excellent cover story."

"I know. And he admitted his alibi for Jasper's murder is weak. Tom said he was at the gym on a free trial day, but no one was tracking who came and went."

Grayson nodded. "Okay. Then we have Patricia Holbrook, a rival wedding planner."

"She lost a lot of business when Vivian moved to town, and even admitted Vivian's death meant an uptick in clients for her."

Grayson asked, 'What was her alibi for Jasper's murder, again?"

"She spoke kind of vaguely about running errands."

Grayson said, "What about Sarah Chen? I hate to think our florist had something to do with this."

"I really don't want to be down a wedding planner, caterer, *and* a florist. At first, I didn't think Sarah could possibly have been involved. Then I found out Vivian had publicly criticized her work, which cost her clients when Vivian pulled in outside florists. After that, I learned Sarah had been floating a sort of 'wedding package deal' with Jasper and Patricia. She wanted to bundle local vendors together. But Jasper and Patricia weren't interested. It sounded like Sarah took Jasper's rejection fairly hard."

"What were her alibis for the murders?" asked Grayson.

"Sarah was at the flower market in Asheville for Vivian's, where she was alone and paid cash. Then for Jasper's, she said she was out making deliveries all day in her van."

The waitress arrived with our plates. My meatloaf was thick and covered in a tomato glaze. The mashed potatoes were whipped totally smooth with a pool of butter melting in the center. I remembered again how hungry I was and quickly tucked into the food.

After a couple of minutes of us enjoying our meals, I said, "Then there's Jessica."

Grayson nodded. "What did you make of her this evening?"

"She's stuck, isn't she? Really stuck. Her whole identity seems wrapped up in her ruined wedding."

Grayson said, "It's like she can't move forward."

"She's almost like Miss Havisham from *Great Expectations*. Except she's stuck on the wedding itself, instead of being jilted at the altar."

Grayson smiled. "It definitely has a very Dickens air to it all."

"Thankfully, she's not wandering around Whitby in her wedding dress." I took a bite of my green beans, which had been cooked slow with bacon, the way only a Southern restaurant could do them. "Tom Cross told me something interesting at the library today. He'd met Jessica's husband here at Quittin' Time a while back. *Ex*-husband, now. Apparently, their marriage didn't survive the wedding disaster. It was annulled."

Grayson's eyebrows rose. "She told us they were working through things."

"I know. Tom said the ex-husband told him Jessica couldn't let it go. That she kept replaying the wedding over and over until he finally left."

Grayson said, "You think Jessica might have blamed Vivian for the end of her marriage?"

"Maybe. Her alibi for Jasper's death wasn't very airtight, was it?"

He shook his head. "Jessica said she was working from home, then took a grocery run."

"But then, no one has an airtight alibi. And everyone had a reason to want Vivian gone. It sounds like Jasper really didn't get much on anyone's bad side, at least not to the extent Vivian had. But he might have realized something later on that made him a target."

Grayson dragged a hush puppy through some tartar sauce. "Right. It sounds like someone was afraid of what he knew or saw." He paused. "How about a new topic? Like our wedding."

I suddenly felt very tired. Maybe it was the heavy comfort of the food I was eating, or maybe the last week was catching up with me. The wedding was now less than two weeks away.

Grayson reached over the table and took my hand. "The last thing I want is for us to be stressing about it. Seriously. I want it to be a joyful, fun day for us. Easy."

"Easy would be nice." I paused. "Any ideas?"

"Yes." He hesitated. "This is unorthodox. It might even sound crazy. And the invitations have gone out, so we'd have to email people or put it on social media."

"What?"

Grayson gave me a wry smile. "We could invent the potluck wedding reception. But we did lose our caterer at zero hour. And if we make the food ourselves, it won't be exactly restful."

I was quiet for a few moments. "That's too funny. Zelda said exactly the same thing. She called it BYOF."

"Bring your own food?"

I laughed. "I didn't take her seriously, but maybe it's a matter of great minds thinking alike."

Grayson said, "It's probably really rude to ask guests to bring food. If we think Emily Post wouldn't approve, we could order pizzas or something."

But I was warming to the idea, unorthodox or not. "Come to think of it, everyone who's coming to the wedding has a sort of specialty, don't they? Mona bakes that incredible pound cake. Luna makes deviled eggs that disappear in five minutes at every library event. Jeremy concocts a mean banana pudding."

Grayson smiled. "I actually love that. It takes all the pressure off and makes everything low-key. And we could still do a few things ourselves. Pick up barbeque take-out or something."

"That's all we need. Good food and good people."

The waitress came by to refill our teas. "Y'all save room for dessert? We've got pecan pie tonight."

Grayson and I exchanged a look.

"Two slices," he said.

A few minutes later, the pie arrived. There were two thick slices with flaky crusts and scoops of vanilla ice cream slowly melting on top. The first bite was sweet and buttery, and the pecans were still slightly warm.

"To simple weddings," Grayson said, lifting his tea.

I clinked mine against it. "To potlucks and pecan pie."

Chapter Twenty-One

I woke up early the next morning, stretching as I sat up in bed. Fitz gave me a lazy, inquiring look.

"No work today," I told him. "But I have birdwatching with Wilson and Mona."

The cat's gaze seemed to wonder what the big deal was. He birdwatched every day from multiple windows.

I scratched him under his chin. "I know you're an expert at birdwatching. I'd bring you along, except I think you might take the opportunity to subdue nature."

Fitz blinked innocently at me.

I got ready, then headed out. I hoped Mona had convinced Wilson to continue their new hobby. It sounded like she'd gotten a lot out of it, and Wilson could definitely use the time in nature as a change of pace.

Mona texted me to say Wilson would drive us all to the trail. I wasn't completely sure I wanted to birdwatch quite as long as they would, but it was very much like Wilson to want to be efficient and take a single car. I told her I'd be ready.

An hour later, a horn tooted outside. Grabbing my water bottle and stuffing it into a small daypack, I hesitated at my purse, then decided I shouldn't need my wallet. I headed out, locking the door behind me.

I spotted binoculars on the front seat as I climbed into the back. "You two look like pros," I said.

"We'll let you borrow the binoculars," said Mona with a smile.

"Hopefully we'll find your pileated woodpecker today," I said. "Although I'm not totally sure I'll recognize it if I do see it."

Wilson seemed to be warming to the birding subject. "You'll know it. It's a big bird with a red crest and a very distinctive call. It sounds almost like laughing."

Mona said, "Like Woody Woodpecker."

"Hmm?" I asked. "Is that another type of woodpecker?"

Mona and Wilson looked at each other. Wilson said sadly, "I forget how young you are, Ann. It's a cartoon bird."

"Never mind," said Mona cheerfully. "We'll find it together."

The parking lot wasn't too busy when Wilson pulled in. A minute later, we were heading up the trail. The crime scene tape had been removed. But I was sure none of us were going to forget anytime soon that Jasper's life had ended right there. The area still felt heavy somehow.

Maybe Mona felt the heaviness, too, because she quickly said, "Look! Was that a nuthatch?"

Wilson lifted his binoculars and concurred. Then he took out a list from his pocket and marked it.

Mona, who seemed determined to keep the mood light, said, "Even though Wilson and I aren't using Patricia Holbrook as our planner. I spoke to a friend of mine on the phone yesterday. She's marrying for a second time and is using her. She said the first meeting with Patricia had gone really well."

I said, "Good. Maybe her business will start picking up soon. You and I wanted to be more in charge of our planning, but Patricia is probably a good fit for plenty of couples."

Mona nodded. "My friend said Patricia seemed to be reining herself in, so maybe she's learning her planning should be more collaborative in nature."

The trail was well-maintained and wide enough for Mona and Wilson to walk side by side. We set out fairly quietly in order to hear calls. Mona pointed them out from time to time, and Wilson checked them off.

"How are the wedding plans going?" I asked in a low tone, not wanting to disturb the birds.

"Very well," said Mona, sounding satisfied. "We're still going with our original plan of the botanical gardens. Simple and beautiful. And I'm glad we're planning everything ourselves, like I mentioned. Patricia might have been a bit too hands-on for our taste. We don't need managing."

Wilson nodded. "We've both perfectly capable of managing ourselves."

"Of course you are," I said.

Wilson stopped suddenly. "There. Hear that? The drumming?"

We all paused, listening. The hammering sound was coming from somewhere in the trees on the side of the trail.

"We must be in the right area," said Wilson. "I'm not sure what type of woodpecker it is, of course."

"Fingers crossed it's our pileated," said Mona. "Let me get out my phone so I can take a picture if it is."

But a few moments later, she said, "Oh, for heaven's sake."

"What's wrong?" I asked.

"I must not have charged my phone last night. I thought I had. Maybe the charger wasn't plugged all the way in. It's totally dead."

Wilson said, "I'll take a picture." He patted his pockets and frowned. "I seem to have left mine in the car."

They both looked at me. I gave them a rueful look in return. "We're a sad group today. I left my phone in my purse, which is back at the house, since I decided to bring a daypack. Oops. I did mean to bring my phone."

They both looked like children who'd heard the magician wasn't coming to their birthday party after all. "I'll head back to the car and grab Wilson's."

"No, I'll go," said Wilson.

"Or we'll all go," said Mona.

"Then you might miss the bird. Even if you don't have your phone, you can at least see it and mark it from your list. I'll be right back."

The trip back down the trail was a lot quicker than the way up. There was a lot less birding going on, for one. I took a deep breath as I approached the area where Jasper had been found. I was going to pass quickly through, but then stopped suddenly as a flash of silver in a sunbeam caught my eye.

There was something metallic poking out of the churned dirt near one of the groundhog holes. It was as if it had been pushed out from below the earth.

It was a bracelet, a small chain with dainty charms. I leaned in closer. One of the charms was a tiny wedding bell.

My breath caught. I remembered the conversation I'd had with Jessica Morton at her house after Vivian's murder. She was a person who spoke with her hands. They were always moving, fidgeting, and being restless. And there had been the soft jangle of that bracelet. I didn't remember seeing it last night, though, when she'd dropped by the newsroom.

I was wondering how the crime scene investigators had missed it when I remembered Wilson mentioning groundhogs on the trail. How they'd get impatient with trash in their homes and would remove it. Had Jessica's bracelet fallen into the groundhog hole when she'd attacked Jasper?

I stood back up from my crouched position, leaving the bracelet where it was. Burton needed to know, and forensics would need to take a look at it. I had to get back to that phone in Wilson's car so I could give him a call.

My mind kept racing. Jasper mentioned rubberneckers and a woman who'd come to the farmhouse at least twice. Had Jessica wanted to return to the scene of her crime? The spot where she'd murdered Vivian?

Something else struck me as I replayed the conversations I'd had with Jessica. She'd said Vivian had set her up with outside catering, but she'd talked about Jasper as if she'd known him. The argument Jasper had witnessed between Vivian and a woman he couldn't quite identify. A woman who'd jabbed her finger at Vivian and had seemed furious.

I hurried across the gravel lot to Wilson's car. There were a couple of other vehicles there. I scanned the lot, his keys in my hand.

And saw Jessica.

Chapter Twenty-Two

Jessica was standing by an older model silver sedan. Her expression shifted when she spotted me. "Ann! What are you doing here?" Her voice was bright.

I kept mine steady. "Oh, birdwatching with friends."

Something in my expression made her frown absently, as if she was trying to understand my mood. "I've been meaning to get out to this trail for ages. It's a good way for me to clear my head. I've heard it's a nice trail with good views." She paused, peering closely at me. "You look pale. Are you okay?"

I forced a smile. "I'm just tired. Maybe it's wedding stress."

"I know. I really do." She took a step forward. "You're getting married pretty soon, aren't you?"

I nodded. "Well, I'd better grab the stuff in the car and join up with my friends again."

"I hope you have a perfect wedding day, Ann."

I smiled tightly at her. "Thanks."

Jessica walked to the trailhead as I got the phone out of the car. I was hoping it wasn't locked so I could make a call. I hadn't realized I was holding my breath until I released it, finding the phone was unlocked. As I dialed Burton's number, I saw Jessica stop still on the trail, stoop, then grab something, slipping it on her wrist. There was a small, satisfied smile on her face.

"Burton, it's Ann. Jessica Morton's bracelet was at Jasper's crime scene. It looked like a groundhog had removed it from its hole. She just found and retrieved it. Can you come over here?"

"On the way," he said grimly, then hung up.

Jessica, despite what she'd said about needing to clear her head, was heading back to her sedan.

I wanted to stall her until Burton arrived. "Decided not to take a walk after all?"

"Oh, I got a text. They need me to fill in for a shift on the phones."

"I see," I said. Then I winced. My tone had been a beat too flat. Or maybe my gaze had strayed to Jessica's wrist, which I'd been valiantly trying not to do.

Jessica's smile faltered, and her eyes narrowed.

"You know, don't you?"

Still trying to stall her, I said slowly, "You left your bracelet here when you attacked Jasper, didn't you? You've been trying to get it back."

Jessica drew in a hissing breath. "You don't know what you're talking about."

"Don't I? Everyone knows your feelings about Vivian. But what I'd like to know is why you killed Jasper. Had he figured something out? Had something been bothering him? Did he confront you?"

Her voice was flat. "He recognized me from that argument I had with Vivian downtown. I guess he didn't recognize me at first, but he did when I saw him at the farmhouse that morning. He was about to set out on his walk but was stretching before he did." Jessica's delivery was matter-of-fact. "I was just chatting with him for a couple of minutes, and he tilted his head to one side. I guess he recognized my voice." She gave a short laugh. "He was so *nice* about it. He said everyone had bad days. That he totally understand why I'd been upset at Vivian, even after all this time had passed. But, you know, he kept asking questions."

The casualness of it hit me like cold water. She was telling me this because she didn't expect me to tell anyone else.

Jessica took a step toward me, and I took one back, tensing.

I blew out a breath I'd been holding as a minivan pulled into the gravel lot. A family spilled out, a mom, dad, a couple of kids, and a golden retriever.

"This is the right trail, isn't it?" the mom asked the dad.

"It's the one with the overlook. I think that's what you wanted."

I quickly walked over to join the family as Jessica watched helplessly. "What a beautiful dog," I said, reaching down to love on the golden retriever, which instantly flopped over on his back, tongue lolling out. I could hear a siren in the distance. Burton was on his way.

When I turned around again, Jessica was in her sedan. A few moments later, she sped off.

The family moved toward the trailhead, and I quickly made another call to Burton. "She peeled out of here in a silver sedan."

"I'm on it," he said grimly before hanging up.

I needed to head back up the trail and rejoin Mona and Wilson. But my legs didn't quite want to move yet. That's when I noticed my hands were trembling. The adrenaline must have been wearing off, leaving something shakier behind it.

I took a slow breath, then took another. I leaned against Wilson's car for a few minutes, thinking. Jasper had figured it out. He'd connected Jessica Morton with the woman he'd seen arguing with Vivian. Then he'd wanted to give Jessica a chance to explain. It was a kindness she didn't deserve, and that had cost him his life.

Taking a deep breath, I pushed myself off the car.

But I didn't even reach the trail when I saw Wilson and Mona coming down it with faces tight with worry.

"Ann? What happened? Are you okay?" asked Mona. "You didn't come back, then we heard a siren."

Wilson was peering at me through his glasses, concern on his face.

"I'm fine." I heard how steady my voice sounded and wondered where that was coming from. "But I found some evidence on the trail near where Jasper was found. I called Burton, and he's handling it."

Wilson studied me for a moment. "You don't look fine. Did the evidence point to anyone in particular?"

"Yes. A woman who'd been a client of Vivian's. Jessica Morton. I'm not sure you'd have known her."

Mona and Wilson looked at each other, then shook their heads.

I must have looked as tired as I sounded because Mona quickly stepped into mother hen mode. "Let's get you home," she said briskly.

I didn't argue.

Wilson glanced at me in the rearview mirror before starting the car. He pulled out his phone. "I need to send a quick text," he said, almost apologetically.

The drive to my house was quiet. Mona filled the silence with gentle chatter, more of a monologue than throwing either Wilson or me the conversational ball. But somehow it made things a little more normal and helped me relax.

When Wilson pulled into my driveway, Grayson's car was already there. He was sitting on my porch steps, brow creased. Wilson cleared his throat. "I thought he'd want to know."

Grayson stood when he saw me. He walked over to give me a quiet hug.

Mona called from the car, "We'll check in later. You get some rest, love."

We walked into the living room. The house was blissfully quiet. I sat down on the sofa, and Fitz immediately claimed my lap, pressing his head firmly against my hand until I scratched behind his ears. His purr started up like a small motor. Grayson busied himself in the kitchen, bringing me a glass of water, a couple of cookies from the jar, and my phone, which I'd told him was still in my purse.

Once he settled next to me, I took a sip of the water, then gave him the short version of what happened. The groundhog hole, the bracelet, Jessica's appearance, her confession, the family arriving, Burton setting out to find Jessica.

Grayson reached out to hold my hand. We sat quietly like that for a few moments. Then he said, "I'm so sorry. That had to have been terrifying."

"I just hope it's all over now. That Burton or the state police has found Jessica. At some point, I'll have to give a statement, I'm sure."

We were still going over what had happened thirty minutes later when there was a tap at my door. It was Burton. looking a bit rumpled and short of breath. "Hey there. I figured I'd drop by instead of making you come to the station to take your statement."

Burton greeted Grayson, then settled in an armchair across from us. Fitz gave him a chirping hello before snuggling again in my lap.

So I gave him the statement, which had birdwatching tangents. I covered the groundhog hole, what little I knew about groundhog habits, the bracelet, the confrontation with Jessica in the parking lot, and the rather miraculous arrival of the family in their van.

After I wrapped up the statement, Burton said, "We got Jessica at her house. She was packing up a bag."

"Did she confess?" asked Grayson.

"Oh, yeah. She totally broke down as soon as we came inside, and she realized it was all over. She spilled everything. Jessica said Jasper figured out what had happened when he saw her near the trail. That made her panic. Apparently, she'd been spending a lot of time near the trail because she was gloating over Vivian's death. It just so happened that Jasper spoke to her this time when he was setting out on his daily walk. I guess, like you're saying Ann, the bracelet was underground since Jasper died. Well, until the groundhog evicted it."

"So basically the groundhog solved the case," said Grayson with a smile.

I said, "Don't tell Wilson. He'll want to give it a library card."

Burton couldn't help but grin at this. "Yep, it's one of the funnier aspects of a not very amusing case. But it definitely helped get things wrapped up. Plus, one of the guys with the state police found Jessica's silver sedan on somebody's security camera, too. It placed her near the farmhouse when Jasper was murdered, even though she'd claimed to be elsewhere. We've got her."

Something in me finally unclenched.

Grayson said, "What information is okay for me to print?"

Burton considered his answer. "You can say an arrest was made and that it was a disgruntled client of Vivian's. Don't name her until we've got formal charges. I'll give you a call when you can write more." He stood up. "Great job with this, Ann. Hope you can get some rest now."

Chapter Twenty-Three

After he left, the cottage felt quieter. Grayson made Earl Grey tea for both of us, the zesty smell filling the quiet room. He sat next to me on the sofa. Fitz was still sound asleep in my lap, a warm, purring weight.

I said, "I keep thinking about what Jessica said to me. She was upset Vivian hadn't even remembered her."

Grayson said, "Vivian hadn't remembered Jessica and the wedding that went wrong?"

"Right. I guess Jessica blended into all the other brides and events Vivian had done. But on Jessica's end, she was totally stuck on that one day. She was furious Vivian had moved on."

Grayson said, "She couldn't let it go."

We sat with that for a while. The afternoon light was softening outside.

"I forgot to tell you I ran into Tom Cross downtown today. I asked him how the job search was going, and he said he got an interview request for next week. He asked me to tell you thanks for the help," said Grayson.

I smiled. "That's good. I think Whitby wasn't much of a good match for him."

"No. But at least now he can move on." Grayson was quiet for a moment. "He looked like a different person. Like he'd actually slept for the first time in weeks. I think the job search was really weighing on him."

"Plus being a suspect in his ex's murder," I said. "When he finds out the investigation is finished, he should feel even more relieved."

I thought about Tom and the first time I'd met him in the park. He'd had those tired eyes, the rumpled appearance, and looked hollowed out by everything that had happened. But then, he'd been dealing with a divorce, losing his job, Vivian's death, and being stuck in a small town that held nothing for him anymore. And, of course, being a suspect on top of it all.

"He feels pretty good about the job lead," said Grayson. "Apparently, he knows someone who works in the department he's applying for."

"That's promising."

We were quiet for a few minutes. A breeze stirred the trees at the edge of the yard, and somewhere in the distance I heard a car door close. Just the ordinary sounds of a regular day.

Then Grayson turned to me, a small smile tugging at the corner of his mouth. "The wedding's in less than two weeks."

"Don't remind me." But I was smiling, too.

"I'm reminding you." His smile widened. "Because for the first time in a while, I think we might actually get there without any more disasters."

I leaned into him, feeling the warmth of his shoulder against mine. He was right. For the first time in days, the wedding felt like something to look forward to again.

The crew finished a week later.

I'd been braced for last-minute disasters like a failed inspection, a delayed delivery, or some construction catastrophe that would leave the addition half-finished on my wedding day. But Eddie called that afternoon, matter-of-fact as always, and said the final walk-through was done.

"You're good to go," he said. "Try not to scuff the floors before Saturday."

That evening, Grayson met me at the cottage. We walked through the new sunroom together, our footsteps echoing on the fresh hardwood. It still smelled like paint and sawdust, that new-construction smell.

I loved seeing the new windows. They were big ones, the kind I'd imagined when we'd first started planning the addition. Through them, I could see the backyard, where the wedding would take place. There was an oak tree, garden beds I needed to tidy up before the wedding, and the patch of grass where we'd set up chairs on Saturday.

"It looks amazing," said Grayson.

I reached out to squeeze his hand.

Fitz padded in behind us, checking out the new space with the air of a building inspector who hasn't yet decided whether to sign off. He sniffed the baseboards, batted experimentally at a dust bunny the crew had missed, then found a patch of late-afternoon sun streaming through one of the big windows. He settled into it immediately, as if he'd been waiting for this spot his whole life.

"I think he approves," said Grayson.

"Which is high praise."

We stood there for a while, not saying much. There would be furniture to arrange later, books to unpack, and decisions about where things should go. But for now, it was enough just to stand in the finished space and let it sink in that we'd actually made it here.

The rest of the week passed by in a blur of last-minute details. Luna stopped by the night before the wedding to help Grayson and me set up chairs. We ended up sitting in several of them, drinking wine and watching the sun go down behind the oak tree.

Holly arrived late Friday night, her car pulling into the driveway right as I was thinking about going to bed. We stayed up too late catching up, the way we always did, and I finally fell asleep around midnight with Fitz curled on my feet.

When I woke up Saturday morning, the cottage already felt alive with activity. Luna had apparently arrived early, and I could hear Holly, who'd stayed in the guest room overnight, talking to her and moving around in the kitchen.

I peered out my window. It was a gorgeous fall day. The sky was a particular October blue; the air was crisp but not cold. It was the kind of day that felt like a gift. We couldn't have ordered one any better.

I heard Luna's voice from downstairs. "Where on earth does she keep the coffee filters? Shouldn't they be next to the coffee?"

Holly said, "I saw them a little while ago when I was looking for a plate. They're above the toaster. No, the other cabinet. There you go."

Fitz brushed up against me, completely unbothered by the commotion downstairs. I gave him a scratch behind his ears. "Ready for this?"

He purred, which I chose to interpret as enthusiasm.

Luna and Holly were both still in the kitchen when I joined them. It looked as if they had transformed the space into command central. There was a checklist on the counter, a garment bag draped over a chair, and what looked like an alarming number of bobby pins spread across the table.

"She's awake!" Luna announced. She was wearing something perfectly Luna, a rust-colored dress with an unexpected print. Her hair was a color it hadn't been a couple of days ago, and there were flowers tucked into it. She looked amazing.

Holly, wearing a demure floral dress, thrust a mug of coffee into my hands. "Good morning, beautiful bride. Drink this. We have a schedule."

"Do we?"

Holly said, "Luna made a spreadsheet."

I looked at Luna. It seemed a very un-Luna-like thing to do.

"It's a very loose spreadsheet," she said with a shrug. "More of a vibe chart. Maybe a mood board." Luna gestured to a chair. "Sit. Breakfast first. That's totally non-negotiable."

Holly set a plate in front of me. It was filled with scrambled eggs, toast, and fresh fruit. I hadn't even realized I was hungry until I saw the food.

"When did you two become a team?" I asked.

"Oh, we've been texting for weeks," said Holly.

"We've been coordinating in a very professional manner," added Luna proudly.

Holly gave me a wry look. "Luna is taking her role very seriously. She even sent me a PowerPoint."

"It was three slides!"

Holly smiled. "One of them was just a photo of Fitz."

"He's an important part of the day."

After breakfast, we started the getting-ready process as the backyard was getting set up for the wedding. The cottage looked different now with the sunroom construction finished and the extra bedroom and library nearly finished. The backyard had been transformed with simple white chairs and Sarah Chen's arrangements everywhere. There were wildflowers, late roses, and sprigs of greenery in mason jars. Nothing fussy at all.

Holly helped supervise. The dress had been hanging in my closet for weeks, and I'd tried not to look at it too often. It felt like looking might somehow jinx something. But now, Holly unzipped the garment bag, and there it was with ivory lace, delicate sleeves, and a modest silhouette. It was the kind of dress that made me feel like myself instead of someone pretending to be a bride.

"It's beautiful," Holly said softly.

Luna nodded. "Very you. Classic without being boring."

"Thanks," I said. "I think."

"That was definitely a compliment."

Holly helped me into the dress while Luna kept Fitz from investigating the trailing hem. There were tiny buttons up the back, and Holly's fingers nimbly worked them.

"Remember when we went dress shopping in Charleston?" Holly asked quietly.

I met her eyes in the mirror. "I remember."

She didn't say anything else about that trip. She didn't need to. Some things had worked out, and other things hadn't. In life, it often seemed to happen that way.

My hair was the next order of business.

"What about this?" Luna held up a sparkly hair clip. It caught the light in approximately seventeen different ways.

"It's very festive," said Holly, tilting her head.

"Festive is good," declared Luna.

"Maybe something simpler? The pearls are already making a statement."

I touched the strand of pearls on my neck. They were my great-aunt's. They served as my something old and helped make me feel my great-aunt was part of my day.

"The pearls are classic," Luna said. "The clip adds a touch of personality."

They carried on for a few minutes. To distract myself, I reached for my book as Luna started telling some random story that had something, perhaps, tangentially to do with hair clips.

A bit later, Holly said, "Now Ann's reading a mystery novel."

Holly and Luna both looked at me.

"I was just checking something," I said, putting the book back down.

"Uh-huh." Luna gently took the book from my hands and set it on the dresser. "Time to get married."

"Fine. But for the record, I was almost at the good part."

"The wedding *is* the good part," said Holly.

In the end, we compromised. Holly did my hair, getting it swept up, elegant, and nothing fussy. Luna contributed a single small hairpin with a tiny crystal that caught the light "just enough."

"There," Holly said, stepping back. "Perfect."

Luna nodded her approval. "Very librarian-bride."

"I'm not sure that's a category," I said.

"It is now. You've invented it."

I looked at myself in the mirror. The dress, the pearls, the simple hair. I looked like me. Only a wedding version of me.

"Well?" Holly asked. "What do you think?"

"I think I'm ready."

"One more thing." Luna produced a length of cream-colored ribbon. "For a furry groomsman."

Fitz, who'd been observing the proceedings from the bed, looked a bit uneasy.

"For Fitz?" asked Holly. "Won't he take off your hand if you try to put it on him?"

"Remember, he's a very laid-back cat," I said. "Very patient."

Luna approached Fitz slowly. He narrowed his eyes a little, but held still as she tied a small bow around his collar. "See? Handsome."

Fitz turned toward the mirror and seemed to agree.

"Just for today," I told him. "Then you can go back to being a regular cat."

"It's about time now," Luna said, glancing at her Mickey Mouse watch.

Holly squeezed my hand. "I'm so happy for you."

"Thanks for being here."

"I wouldn't have missed it for the world." She smiled. "Besides, someone had to make sure you didn't spend your wedding morning solving a mystery."

From outside, I heard the sound of cars arriving, full of guests.

Luna said, "I'm going to check on the reception setup in the backyard. I'll make sure Zelda hasn't rearranged the food table."

"Is that a concern?"

"With Zelda, everything is always a concern." Luna paused at the door. "You look amazing, by the way. Grayson's going to lose it."

Then she was gone, her rust-colored dress disappearing down the hall.

A minute later, there was a knock at the bedroom door. It was Wilson, looking unusually nervous in his best suit. He was still formal, still Wilson, but with something a little softer in his expression. "They're ready for us," he said. Then, a little quieter, "Are you ready, too?"

I took a breath. Through the window, I could see the backyard, full of chairs, flowers, and the people I loved, all gathered together.

I took his arm. We headed for the door. Fitz padded after us, his ribbon slightly askew, as if he'd already tried and failed to remove it.

Wilson and I walked down the aisle, which was just a path through chairs in the backyard, with Grayson next to Jeremy, waiting at the end. As I walked with Wilson, I had a blur of impressions. Mona was dabbing her eyes, already crying happy tears even though the wedding had barely started. Linus was in his customary suit, sitting very straight. Zelda sat next to him, looking almost soft. Timothy and Owen were near the back, Owen craning to see everything. Burton, sitting next to his girl-friend Belle, gave me a grin.

Fitz was stationed in a chair near the front, watching the proceedings with smiling green eyes.

And then there was Grayson. He was looking at me as if I were the only person in the yard. Like the murders and chaos and the construction delays all led to exactly this moment. I reached him, and Wilson placed my hand into Grayson's before stepping back. His hand was warm and steady around mine.

The ceremony was short and simple, which was exactly what we'd wanted. Pastor Richards had known my great-aunt, had known me since I was a little girl, and having him there lent a full circle feel to the day. There was a reading about love being patient and kind, which made Luna sniffle behind me. Some-where in the middle, Fitz let out a small chirp, and a quiet ripple of laughter moved through the guests.

When it came time for the vows, Grayson's voice was clear and sure. Mine was a little shakier than I'd expected, but I meant every word.

And then Pastor Richards smiled and told Grayson he could kiss the bride. He did, and the yard erupted in applause and a few cheerful whoops from Jeremy and Luna.

The reception spilled across the yard in the warm afternoon light. Someone had strung fairy lights through the trees. Every-thing was golden with the autumn leaves, the late roses in Sarah's arrangements, and the smiles on everyone's faces.

Zelda had set up her chicken and dumplings at the center of the food table, presiding over it like a general surveying her troops. As she'd promised, she'd also brought me a batch far prior to the wedding. It had been as delicious as she'd proclaimed.

"It's my grandmother's recipe," I heard her telling Linus. "None of that store-bought broth nonsense."

Linus nodded gravely, accepting a generous portion. "It smells extraordinary."

"Of course it does."

The potluck had come together better than I could have imagined. There were casseroles and salads and Luna's deviled eggs. A platter of Jasper's biscuits sat near the end of the table, which his sister had provided from his recipe. It felt right having something of his here with us.

Grayson squeezed my hand. "Hungry?"

"Starving, actually."

We made our way through the food line together, plates in hand, stopping every few feet to accept hugs and congratulations. Burton and Belle were talking with Wilson and Mona near the punch bowl. Burton was looking almost relaxed, which was nice to see.

Timothy and Owen were hovering near the dessert table, eating plenty of cookies and brownies. Nearby, Zelda was watching them with a look that was almost soft, though she'd deny it if anyone mentioned it.

Luna swept by with Jeremy, their hands linked. Since he'd been offered the job position remotely, they'd decided to stay in Whitby, at least for now.

"Best wedding ever," Luna said, pulling me into a one-armed hug without letting go of Jeremy.

"You might be biased."

"Absolutely not. I'm extremely objective." She grinned. "Also, I'm taking credit for the ribbon on Fitz. He looks very handsome."

Fitz, for his part, had abandoned his chair and was making the rounds, accepting chin scratches and admiration from all.

Someone put on music, something warm and easy. A few couples started dancing on the grass. Wilson led Mona out with the kind of formal care that made her laugh and lean into him.

Grayson and I found a quiet moment on the edge of the yard, looking back at the cottage. It was a home for both of us now, with its new addition and its fairy lights and the people we loved still milling around both inside and out.

"Worth the wait?" Grayson asked.

"Every bit of it."

About the Author

Bestselling cozy mystery author Elizabeth Spann Craig is a library-loving, avid mystery reader. A pet-owning Southerner, her four series are full of cats, corgis, and cheese grits. The mother of two, she lives with her husband, a fun-loving corgi, and a couple of cute cats.

Sign up for Elizabeth's free newsletter to stay updated on releases:

https://bit.ly/2xZUXqO

This and That

I love hearing from my readers. You can find me on Facebook as Elizabeth Spann Craig Author, on Twitter as elizabethscraig, on my website at elizabethspanncraig.com, and by email at elizabethspanncraig@gmail.com.

Thanks so much for reading my book...I appreciate it. If you enjoyed the story, would you please leave a short review on the site where you purchased it? Just a few words would be great. Not only do I feel encouraged reading them, but they also help other readers discover my books. Thank you!

Did you know my books are available in print and ebook formats? Most of the Myrtle Clover series is available in audio and some of the Southern Quilting mysteries are. Find the audiobooks here: https://elizabethspanncraig.com/audio/

Please follow me on BookBub for my reading recommendations and release notifications.

I'd also like to thank some folks who helped me put this book together. Thanks to my cover designer, Karri Klawiter, for her awesome covers. Thanks to my editor, Judy Beatty for her help. Thanks to beta readers Amanda Arrieta, Rebecca Wahr, Cassie Kelley, and Dan Harris for all of their helpful suggestions and careful reading. Thanks to my ARC readers for helping to spread the word. Thanks, as always, to my family and readers.

Other Works by Elizabeth

Myrtle Clover Series in Order (be sure to look for the Myrtle series in audio, ebook, and print):

Pretty is as Pretty Dies

Progressive Dinner Deadly

A Dyeing Shame

A Body in the Backyard

Death at a Drop-In

A Body at Book Club

Death Pays a Visit

A Body at Bunco

Murder on Opening Night

Cruising for Murder

Cooking is Murder

A Body in the Trunk

Cleaning is Murder

Edit to Death

Hushed Up

A Body in the Attic

Murder on the Ballot

Death of a Suitor

A Dash of Murder
Death at a Diner
A Myrtle Clover Christmas
Murder at a Yard Sale
Doom and Bloom
A Toast to Murder
Mystery Loves Company
A Murder Down Memory Lane
Murder Sees All
Volunteer for Murder
The Village Library Mysteries in Order:
Checked Out
Overdue
Borrowed Time
Hush-Hush
Where There's a Will
Frictional Characters
Spine Tingling
A Novel Idea
End of Story
Booked Up
Out of Circulation
Shelf Life
Dead Silence
Plot Twist
Final Draft
The Sunset Ridge Mysteries in Order
The Type-A Guide to Solving Murder
The Type-A Guide to Dinner Parties

The Type-A Guide to Book Clubs
The Type-A Guide to Holiday Home Tours (2026)

Southern Quilting Mysteries in Order:
Quilt or Innocence
Knot What it Seams
Quilt Trip
Shear Trouble
Tying the Knot
Patch of Trouble
Fall to Pieces
Rest in Pieces
On Pins and Needles
Fit to be Tied
Embroidering the Truth
Knot a Clue
Quilt-Ridden
Needled to Death
A Notion to Murder
Crosspatch
Behind the Seams
Quilt Complex
A Southern Quilting Cozy Christmas

MEMPHIS BARBEQUE MYSTERIES in Order (Written as Riley Adams):
Delicious and Suspicious
Finger Lickin' Dead

Hickory Smoked Homicide

Rubbed Out

And a standalone "cozy zombie" novel: Race to Refuge, written as Liz Craig